Books by Giles Tippette

Fiction

THE BANK ROBBER
THE TROJAN COW
THE SURVIVALIST
THE SUNSHINE KILLERS
AUSTIN DAVIS
WILSON'S WOMAN
WILSON YOUNG ON THE RUN
THE TEXAS BANK ROBBING COMPANY
WILSON'S GOLD
WILSON'S REVENGE
WILSON'S CHOICE
WILSON'S LUCK
HARD LUCK MONEY
CHINA BLUE
BAD NEWS
CROSS FIRE
JAILBREAK
HARD ROCK
SIXKILLER
GUNPOINT
DEAD MAN'S POKER
CHEROKEE

Nonfiction

THE BRAVE MEN
SATURDAY'S CHILDREN
DONKEY BASEBALL AND OTHER SPORTING DELIGHTS
I'LL TRY ANYTHING ONCE

THE SUNSHINE KILLERS

GILES TIPPETTE

JOVE BOOKS, NEW YORK

This book contains the complete text of the original edition. It has been completely reset in a typeface designed for easy reading and was printed from new film.

THE SUNSHINE KILLERS

A Jove Book / published by arrangement with the author

PRINTING HISTORY
First edition published August 1975
Jove edition / February 1995

ISBN: 0-515-11535-5

A JOVE BOOK®
Jove Books are published by The Berkley Publishing Group, 200 Madison Avenue, New York, New York 10016. JOVE and the "J" design are trademarks belonging to Jove Publications, Inc.

PRINTED IN THE UNITED STATES OF AMERICA

10 9 8 7 6 5 4 3 2 1

To my wife,
Beverly

THE SUNSHINE KILLERS

ONE

THROUGH THE FADING moments of a bleak, cold winter day, a lone horseman came riding slowly across the snow-covered high country of northern Arizona. It was rough land, broken and rocky looking even under its heavy load of snow, with high plateaus and mountains rising far off in the distance. A light snow was still falling and it swirled and blew in hard gusts around the rider and his horse. He rode in the posture of a man who was tired and cold and discouraged, slightly slumped in the saddle, letting the motion of the horse swing and jog his body. They moved gingerly, the horse seeming to pick his own way more than by the guide of the man. Occasionally they would stop as they topped a little rise and the man would ease himself up straighter and take long looks around. He had his hat pulled low and the collar of his big coat turned up, but still his face was red and cold looking from the wind and the blowing snow. Once he worked his hand inside his coat and grimaced as he felt his ribs. When he took it out he looked at his glove as if expecting to see something on it.

They kept plodding along, the sun getting lower and lower in the leaden sky. Its bottom rim was just touching the far-off horizon when the rider urged his horse up a long incline, the animal floundering and kicking through the powdery

1

snow, and stopped at the crest. Before him lay a long valley, soft and welcome looking under its deceptive mantle of snow. In the middle of the valley were several buildings, a little town. Smoke, rising from a few rock chimneys, disappeared quickly into the snowy haze of the sky. It was a bleak scene, this little town in the middle of nowhere, but the rider suddenly urged his horse forward, spurring him hard to make the tired animal move, and began the long descent.

Now the winter darkness was coming fast, seeming to almost be racing the rider into the town. But at the edge of the settlement the rider paused by a wooden sign mounted on a fence post. Drifting snow had partially covered the face of the sign and he leaned down and swiped it away with a gloved hand. Burned into the wood was the name of the town, SUNSHINE, ARIZONA TERRITORY. The rider looked at it for a long moment without smiling. Finally he turned his face up to the falling snow for just a second and then put spurs to his horse and started in.

He was erect now in the saddle, riding cautiously, looking constantly to his left and right as he passed down the street between the few buildings. He pulled up in front of what appeared to be a combination general store and saloon. A single sign, creaking forlornly in the wind, announced the place as "Schmidt's." The rider looked at it a moment, wiped a tired hand across his face and then rode his horse around on the windward side of the building so that the animal would be out of the wind and somewhat protected from the cold. He dismounted stiffly, and tied the reins to a post.

Moving as if in pain, he loosened the saddle girth and then got a feed bag from his duffel tied behind the dish of the saddle and put it over the horse's head, working carefully to make sure the straps were properly fitted and that it would stay in place. Lastly he pulled a long, heavy rifle out of the boot on the left side of the saddle. The rifle was encased in a fringed, beaded case that was darkened with grease and use. Holding the rifle in his right hand he walked slowly around the store and stepped up on the porch. He was dressed in a heavy fleece-lined coat that came nearly to his knees, buffalo leggings, and a broad-brimmed, low-crowned hat. He paused outside the door to try and brush off some of the snow, taking off his hat and beating it at his coat and leggings. As he stamped his boots against the wooden floor of the porch you could hear the faint jingle of his big Mexican spurs. Then, just before opening the door, he put on his hat and unbuttoned his coat, pulling it back slightly so that the big pistol at his belt would be clear.

He didn't go freely into the saloon. Instead he stepped through the door and then stopped, easing the door closed behind him as he took a long second to look around. Standing there he was a tall, lean man with a certain gauntness about his face that could have come from tiredness or disappointment or too much pain, or all of that. By his posture you could see that he was tired, dead tired, but in spite of that there was still the set and carriage about him of a proud, capable man.

The saloon was smoky and dim. At first all he

could make out clearly was the owner behind the bar, Schmidt. He was a fat, powerful-looking man with a full beard wearing a dirty white apron. He stared blankly at the man at the door. The stranger looked at him and then let his gaze shift around the room. Now his eyes were adjusting and he could make out two tables full of rough-looking men. Whatever talk had been going on had stopped at his entrance. They all stared at him openly. One, leaning back in his chair with his boots up on the table, his spurs digging into the wood, turned his head and spit without taking his eyes off the man at the door.

Further back, near the huge fireplace which was roaring and smoking, there were one or two more figures, but they were indistinct to the stranger in the gloom. One part of the saloon was sectioned off as a general store and you could see supplies, such as sacks of flour and cured bacon hanging from the ceiling, and ropes and other paraphernalia a man might need in such country.

Finally he walked slowly over to the bar, which was nothing but rough planks laid over upright barrels. He still had the huge rifle in his hand and he looked carefully around one more time before leaning it up against the bar. "Whiskey," he said in a low voice.

"You want the good stuff or the ordinary?"

The man seemed to consider. "What's the difference?"

"Five cents the shot."

"Just the ordinary."

The bartender poured him out a shot and the man downed it, grimacing slightly at the taste.

Schmidt waited expectantly, the opened bottle still in his hand. The man made a motion and Schmidt poured him out another drink. He knocked off half that and then set his glass back down on the bar. The whiskey was warming him and he seemed to relax slightly. The bartender, seeing he was not going to be drinking that fast, corked the bottle and set it on the bar.

"That's forty cents," he said.

The man made a tired motion with his hand, then reached in a pocket and brought out a silver dollar. He put it carefully on the bar in front of him.

At that moment a dark young man in ragged clothes came edging up from the dim back. "Say, you buy me wheesky?"

"Goddamit, Chiffo!" the bartender yelled. "Git away!"

With his slouch hat he leaned over the bar and beat the young man back. "Get on back in that corner and don't bother none of these folks or I'll throw you out in the snow!"

The young man retreated and the bartender grumbled, "Damn half-breed, don't know why I let him hang around the place."

Not looking, not even seeming to see, the man reached out and uncorked the bottle of whiskey. Using only one hand he uprighted a glass and poured out a full shot. Still using just the one hand, his right, he corked the bottle and put the full glass near the edge of the bar. In a move so slow that it seemed to hurt, he looked over to where the half-breed had gone to huddle near the fire. "Hey," he said hoarsely, "come here." He made a motion toward the whiskey. The half-breed rushed forward, an apprehensive eye on the bartender, grabbed the glass, and downed the whiskey.

"Now ain't that something," Schmidt said sourly. "For what you spent on a drink for that lizard-edged bastard you could have been drinkin' the good stuff. Well, that's sixty cents."

The man said, in a tired whisper, as if explanation, "It's cold. Cold."

"And going to get a damned sight colder," Schmidt told him.

"It can't," the man answered. As if he'd suddenly felt the temperature, he hunched himself up, drawing the whiskey to his mouth and gulping at it. It seemed to warm him for he took off his broad-brimmed hat and laid it on the bar. "Is there a stable for my horse?"

For a moment Schmidt seemed to have not heard the question, then he asked, "What?" The man repeated it and the bartender shifted uneasily and then shook his head. "No, no stable." He took up a cloth and began to wipe the rough top of the plank.

The man frowned. He had been in the act of picking up the bottle of whiskey, but now he set it back down. "What do you mean? I saw a barn out back."

"No stable," Schmidt said again. "And no lodging. No room. All filled up." He glanced over the stranger's shoulder at the little group of men around the near table.

The stranger straightened slowly. He looked hard at Schmidt, a curious expression in his eyes.

"And I saw a bunkhouse out back. It can't be full." He turned and looked behind him, his eyes going slowly from one man to another. "I don't have to have a bed. Just out of the cold. But my horse has got to have shelter."

"All full," Schmidt said again.

The stranger turned back to him. He said carefully, "I don't think you'd turn a man away on a night like this. I don't think that'd be right." He stared at Schmidt. He knew something was wrong somewhere, but he couldn't find it. From the way Schmidt kept glancing toward the men at the tables he knew it had to involve them. He could feel a little rush of energy and strength as his body instinctively got ready for the trouble he could feel. He said, distinctly, so that his words would carry throughout the room, "You will need an awful good reason to put a man out on a night like this. It better be one I can understand and I haven't heard yet."

Schmidt didn't answer, he just stood there staring over the stranger's shoulder. Finally there was a voice, from the near table. "Put him up, Schmidt. For tonight."

The man turned slowly, to see who'd spoken. For a moment he studied the faces around the table, then settled on a pleasant-looking young cowboy. For a brief flicker the cowboy seemed to have nodded and the stranger turned back to the bar. Schmidt said, "All right. Keep for your horse is a dollar. You get bed and board for fifty cents."

The man smiled faintly at this logic and the bartender explained sharply. "Hay has gone to a hundred dollars a ton and none to be had. Men are cheap in this country. It costs to feed a horse."

"I'll take it," he said.

"Dollar and a half."

The man put two dollars on the bar. "I'll drink out the change."

"Chiffo!" the bartender yelled. "Get your worthless ass out there and put up the man's horse."

The boy scurried out.

The man took another drink and then said softly, "Sunshine."

Schmidt looked at him. "What?"

"I was just wondering at the name of your town. Sunshine."

At that one of the men at the table, the one with his feet up, a short, unpleasant-looking man, said, "You don't like the name of our town?"

The man at the bar turned slightly sideways. He didn't speak.

"I ast you a question. You don't like the name of our town?"

"I don't care one way or another," the stranger said.

The short, chunky man brought his feet to the floor with a thump. He smiled, but it was not pleasant. "Why, then, don't let us keep you where you don't want to be. You don't like this town, ride on."

The man looked at him, a little frown lowering his eyes.

Tension was suddenly heavy in the air. The pleasant-faced cowboy abruptly said, "Oh hell, Tomlain, have a drink. Let the man alone."

Tomlain raised his voice slightly. "Where you from, boy, that you come around knockin' the name of other folks' towns? Where'd you learn that?"

The man looked levelly at Tomlain, not at all concerned by the man's obvious forcing.

"South."

With that he turned back to the bar and took down the rest of his drink. Then he shook himself as if shrugging off a bad feeling. As the life slowly worked its way back into his face you could see, rough, beat down and haggard though he was, that he was not some rode-out wanderer voyaging through the land. There was a distinguished quality about his face, a gentleness in his eyes, an aristocratic aloofness and aloneness that set him apart from the ordinary run of men. He was dressed no different, nor looked much different from the other men in the room, but there was a presence and quality about him that he, himself, knew about and which they immediately recognized. This quality awed and befriended some men, others it antagonized because they recognized themselves as being inferior to such a person and they felt they must somehow find a way to trample on him and bring him down.

The bartender had been looking at the big rifle the man had leaning against the bar. "That's some cannon," he finally commented. "Sharps?"

"Special built," the man answered.

"You a hunter?"

"I have been."

"What's the caliber of that weapon?"

"Big enough," the man said.

"What do you hunt with it?"

The man didn't answer. Instead he finished his glass of whiskey and asked, "The bunkhouse?"

The bartender nodded. "I take it you've got your own bedroll."

"Yes," the man said.

"We furnish extra blankets for a price. The lice are free."

The man smiled slightly and started for the door. As he walked Tomlain called to him. "Is that a real rifle you got in that pretty Indian case, boy?"

The man glanced at him and kept walking.

Tomlain persisted. "We supposed to believe you can shoot a gun like that?"

The man went on out.

When he had gone, Billy, the pleasant-faced cowboy, looked at Tomlain, and shook his head. "What do you want to go stirring up that pilgrim for?"

"I didn't like him," Tomlain answered. "And anyway, he ain't supposed to be here." He called to Schmidt. "What'd you let him stay for, Schmidt? McGraw bought this whole goddam town. He ain't going to like no strangers around."

Schmidt pointed at Billy. "He said it was all right."

Billy turned to Tomlain. "Mister McGraw also said not to draw no notice. You don't run a man out in the snow on a freezing night, not at a public inn. And you sure don't pick a fight with him."

"Well, I don't like it," Tomlain growled. "And I'm going to find out that pilgrim's business. What's he doing here, anyway?"

Billy made a disgusted sound. "You just don't like it because he had that sharpshooter's rifle. You don't like anyone you think could shoot as good as you. Tomlain, you ain't the only rifle shot in the world."

Tomlain looked at him and took a drink of whiskey. "I ought to run him off. Or kill him."

"He'll be gone in the morning," Billy said.

Outside, the man trudged slowly through the snow, watching out from under his hat, as the half-breed took his horse into the stable. The bunkhouse was a long, adobe building with tiny windows and a pole roof chinked in with more adobe. The man went in. There were eight or ten bunks lined up on each side of the room: wooden frames with rawhide strips for springs and no mattresses. The man sank down tiredly on the nearest one. For a moment he didn't move. Finally he heaved himself and removed his big coat. Still as if in slow motion he unbuttoned his shirt and pulled up the heavy underwear he was wearing underneath. His left side was heavily bandaged. The bandage was stained with dried blood. He touched it gingerly and grimaced. The wound was about midway down his left side. It was a gunshot wound and, from the way the man moved, you could tell it might have broken a rib or two. He touched it again, exploring the painful area with sensitive fingers, then pulled his underwear down and buttoned his shirt. At that moment the half-breed came in with his bedroll. He came up and laid it at the foot of the man's bed. "I see your horse is feexed up good," the boy said.

The man nodded. "There's a drink still coming in the money I left at the bar. Tell Schmidt I said you were to have it." He went slowly to his pocket and brought out another silver dollar. "Go get me whatever piece of a bottle that will buy and some tobacco."

The boy took the money, but stood there looking at him for a second. "You seek?"

"No," the man said. "Go on."

When the boy had left, the man spread the bedroll out on the cot, putting his big rifle in at the side. He bothered to take off his boots, the effort obviously painful, then sat down on the bed and laid back. Lying there he took his big pistol out of the holster, saw to its loading, then slipped it in his belt. Then he lay there staring at the ceiling, waiting for the boy to come back with the whiskey in hopes that it would dull the pain of the gunshot wound in his side.

Morning came swiftly. The snow had ceased and the sun was out. Its beams, shining through the small windows of the dim bunkhouse, were like rays from a lantern, cutting sharply through the smoke and the dark air. The man came awake all at once, aware that there were men standing around him. Three, all from the evening before, were there, just at the end of his bunk, staring at him silently. Instinctively his hand went to the gun in his belt, then relaxed as he saw they didn't have weapons out. Then he noticed that his shirt was open and his undershirt pulled up, exposing the bandage. The wound had been bleeding afresh and someone had seen it and investigated. His eyes went quickly from face to face; he recognized two of them, Tomlain and Billy. Tomlain was the nearest, standing just to the right. Billy was at the foot of the bed. When he saw that the man was awake he grinned and said, "Going to sleep all day?"

But the man made no sign; he was watching Tomlain, noting that he was wearing a pistol set up for someone who might want to get at it in a hurry. Tomlain suddenly leaned over and, with an ungentle finger, jabbed the man in his wound. "Where'd you get that, boy?" he asked.

The man flinched, but made no sound. Instead his eyes got very hard. His hand was still resting just off the butt of the pistol in his belt. Billy said, "Don't do that, Tomlain. You can see it hurts him."

"I ain't worryin' about that," Tomlain said. He licked his lips and grinned. "I want to know what done it. I want a few answers off our old buddy boy here."

The man, still without showing any sign of emotion, hitched himself up further on the bed so that he was no longer lying flat. He could feel a surge of preparation run through him. Billy, recognizing it, said, "Don't be doing that." He said it almost kindly, but there was a definite threat in his voice. "We just want to know a little about you." He paused, and, getting no response, added, "We got a reason. See, we don't want no trouble."

But Tomlain reached down again and prodded at the wound. "That's a gunshot wound, ain't it?"

In a move so swift that it seemed almost casual, the man knocked Tomlain's hand away and then half pulled the pistol out of his belt. He didn't pull it all the way for there were three of them and they were the kind of men, in that time and in that country, who, if you pulled a pistol, would have pulled their own and started shooting. The man did not take hold of his pistol as a threat, but only as a warning. He'd calculated the move to just the right degree and they recognized that.

"Come now," Billy said. "None of that now. We just want to talk to you."

"Hell with that, Billy," Tomlain said, his voice rising. "I want to know who the bastard is and what his business is. I don't want him bringin' no storm down round my ears."

"See," Billy explained, "we got some folks around here who get nervous about unusual things goin' on. That's why we just want to ask you a few questions. Hope you'll take it the right way. What's your name?"

The man looked from face to face for a second. Finally he answered, "Name's Saulter."

"Where you come from, Mister Saulter?"

"South," the man said.

"We know that," Billy answered patiently. "What we mainly want to know is what's your business in Sunshine and how come you here?"

The man looked at the three faces slowly. Finally he said in that hoarse whisper, "I need a rest. This place was here . . . I just stumbled on it."

"Listen," Tomlain broke in angrily, "this won't get it." He pointed at Saulter's wound. "Somebody shot you and you're running. What we want to know is are they chasing you? Have you got somebody fixing to come in here with company we don't want to see?"

Saulter was a long time answering. Finally he shook his head slowly. "No," he said, "nobody is chasing me. Not now."

Tomlain made a sneering sound. "Sure, Pilgrim, we believe you. That's why you're running with a bullet in you. If you ain't being chased, why are you on the jump?"

"It's a long story."

"Well, we want to hear it. We got plenty of time."

The man shook his head and lay back tiredly, ignoring Tomlain's remark.

Tomlain started to make a move but Billy restrained him. "Aw, let him be, Tomlain. Let him rest a bit, we can take it up with him later. Let's get some breakfast."

He took the unwilling Tomlain by the arm and pulled him away. But, as they went out, the short gunman turned to look back at Saulter, his leer a promise of more to come.

When they were gone, Saulter swung around and sat on the side of the bed. Slowly, he pulled his undershirt down and buttoned his shirt. In spite of the fire at the far end of the bunkhouse it was still cold and his breath steamed in the air. First he put on his hat and then shrugged into his big coat. He had to rest before he could struggle into his boots. When he was dressed he still sat on his bed, seeming too done in to move just yet. At that moment the half-breed came in with a load of firewood. He carried it down to the fireplace and threw it in, causing sparks and coals to come flying out. Then he came back up to Saulter. "Maybe you buy me one wheesky?"

Saulter didn't move for a second. Finally he reached under the bed and came out with a bottle. He sighted it against the light. There was about an inch left. He uncorked it, took a long drink, then handed the rest to Chiffo. While the boy was drinking, Saulter located the stump of a thin black cigar and lit it. He smoked meditatively for a moment. The boy watched him.

"Who are those men?" Saulter asked.

The boy shrugged. "Just some mens."

"Do they stay or do they go?"

"They stay."

"What do they do around here? Do they work? Are they hunters? Prospectors?"

"They don't work. They just stay."

"How long they been here?"

The boy shrugged. "Pretty long."

"A week? A month?"

"I don't know. Pretty long. They don't buy me no wheesky."

"They just sit around here all day?"

"I think," the boy said, "that they're pretty bad men. Yes, I think maybe they pretty bad. I think maybe they already kill one man maybe two."

"What for? Did they rob him?"

"Who can say? Maybe they kill somebody. Maybe not." The boy's face suddenly brightened. "You buy me more drink of wheesky?"

"Not now," Saulter said. "You go on."

After the boy was gone Saulter reached in his pocket and took out a little deerskin shot bag. He emptied the contents in his hand. It was all the money he had and he counted it laboriously. Then he clinked it meditatively in his hand. After a second he put it back in the bag and the bag back in his pocket. He sat there thinking that he needed to rest and recuperate, but that he wouldn't be able to do it long in such a place on eight dollars. Well, there really had been no reason for him to have only eight dollars. His pride had been the only reason. But it was too late for that now. Then he sat awhile longer, thinking about this place, this Sunshine town. There was something going on here, something he didn't quite understand. He was not curious about it except as it applied to himself, but the hell of it was that it looked as if it were going to involve him. They didn't want him here. They'd made that plain. For whatever reason. But he was hurt and he was going to have to stop off awhile until he healed. But they'd said one night. That was what the man behind him, at the table, Billy he guessed it was, had told the bartender. Well, he couldn't leave. It was a long way to nowhere across that frozen desert and neither he nor his horse were up to it yet.

So, he guessed, there'd be trouble. He didn't understand it and he probably wouldn't understand it when it came, but he'd handle it. The image of Tomlain ran through his through his mind. He'd seen his kind in camps and bars all over the country. The man wouldn't quit pushing until it came down to guns. He expected he'd have to kill Tomlain. He might have it out with all of them if it came to that, but he hoped not. He tried to think how many there were. There'd been three that morning, but there were others. Five or six, he guessed. Well, he was in kind of a fix, a little bit of a tight place. For whatever reason, they seemed too set on making him leave, but they ought to realize that he couldn't. He'd walk as quietly as he could, but he didn't think it was going to do much good.

He got up and left the bunkhouse and went in the store. The others were there and he took a table in a corner, off by himself. They watched him steadily, all of them. From behind the bar Schmidt called to ask if he wanted coffee. "Yes," Saulter said. He got out one of the little thin, black cigars and lit it, the strong smoke biting him deep in the lungs. Through it he could see Tomlain watching him, not taking his eyes off him even when he turned his head to spit.

When Schmidt brought his coffee, he asked what he could have to eat for breakfast.

"Beans," the owner said. "Or bacon."

"Do you have any eggs?"

Schmidt laughed, loudly. "Did you hear that?" he called to the other men. "He wants eggs."

"Tell him to go lay one," Tomlain said.

Saulter did not respond. He sat there, not looking at anything particular, breathing shallowly because his ribs hurt otherwise. The wound itself hadn't been so bad; it had missed his lungs by a good inch or two. If it just hadn't broken those two ribs. It pulled him down, wore him out.

Schmidt finally brought his food and, as he sat there eating the poor fare, Billy got up from the group at the table, coffee cup in hand, and came over and sat down. "Mind if I visit a minute?" he asked.

Saulter, busy with a mouthful of bacon, just shook his head. He had been expecting something ever since he'd come in. He was just hopeful it would hold off long enough for him to eat.

Billy sat there for a long moment, watching Saulter eat, taking little sips of his coffee. Finally he said, "I guess you'll be moving on, won't you? Right after you finish your breakfast?"

"No."

Billy shook his head and smiled slightly. "I think it'd be a good idea. Can't be nothing about Sunshine to attract you."

Saulter said, "I need the rest." He was willing to go that far, to explain.

Billy nodded. "Your wound. I understand." He jerked his head toward the other table. "Listen, I'm sorry about the way old Tomlain acted. Over at the bunkhouse. That's just his way. He's about as bred up as a common goat."

Saulter nodded.

Billy scratched his chin and glanced over at Saulter's rifle. It was leaning against the table, right at Saulter's side. "That thing's big as a cannon. It go everywhere with you?"

Saulter nodded. He was about finished eating.

"You don't talk much, do you?"

"It hurts to talk," Saulter said lowly.

"Ah," Billy said. "Your ribs. Must have one busted. How about a good laugh? Reckon that'd feel good? What if I was to tell you some real funny jokes?"

Saulter smiled faintly. He knew that Billy was

being friendly for a purpose. He just wished he'd get on with whatever it was he'd come over to say.

"Heard you to say you was a hunter. Reckon what kind?"

"Contract," Saulter said in a hoarse whisper. "I was a contract hunter for the railroads they're building."

"Railroads?" Billy looked startled. He glanced over at the table where the men were sitting, watching and listening. "The continental hook-up? I thought they was a good little piece from here."

"They're getting closer," Saulter said. He pushed back his plate and then picked up the stump of the cigar he'd been smoking. Before he could light it, Billy reached in his shirt pocket, pulled out a long cigar, and tossed it across to Saulter. "Here," he said, "have a fresh one. That one looks like it's been rode hard and put up wet."

Saulter nodded and picked up the cigar. He took a careful moment to light it. When he had it drawing good, he leaned back in his chair. "Thanks."

They stared at each other for a half moment.

Finally Billy grinned. "Well, tell me, Mister Saulter, if I ain't prying, how come you leave off working for the railroads. I'd think that would be pretty good employ."

Saulter considered the question for a moment, turning the cigar in his mouth and looking at the four men at the other table. "It was their choice," he said finally.

"Have anything to do with that?" Billy asked, gesturing toward Saulter's wound.

Again Saulter spent a long moment considering the question. It was pushing his privacy, but then there was something going on here he hadn't got all figured out. "It was a fair fight," he said.

Billy laughed. "Sounds like you was hunting the wrong kind of game."

"It was a fair fight," Saulter said again. He raised his voice, speaking now for the benefit of the whole room. There was a menace in his words. "A man put me in a corner and wouldn't leave me no way out except to kill him. It was his mistake."

It brought a silence. Billy looked at him. He understood what Saulter meant and what he was saying.

Saulter took the cigar from his mouth and put it out. "Now I'm a little curious," he said to Billy. He jerked his head toward the other table. "How come you and that bunch are pushing me so hard toward the city limits?"

Billy smiled and shrugged. "Well, we just can't understand why you'd want to hang around Sunshine, Mister Saulter. Ain't much here."

"I told you why," Saulter said evenly.

"Well, that worries us, Mister Saulter," Billy admitted. "See, we're worried you might have got in some trouble with the law and there might be a whole pack of them right behind fixing to come piling in here on us. And we wouldn't like that. So we'd kind of like them to see your trail leading out the other side of town. Understand what I mean?"

"I told you nobody was tracking me. I'm not wanted. By nobody."

"Yes, that's what you *told* us, Mister Saulter. Still and all."

"All I can do is tell you."

Billy put a cigar between his teeth and smiled around it. "I reckon I might say some of the same if I was wounded and needed a place to hole up. But, see, we might be wanted men, for all you know. You could understand how we'd feel then."

Saulter looked at Billy and then at the other men. "If you're wanted," he said slowly, "they'd be tracking you, not me."

"Still," Billy said.

Saulter looked at him. "Is it just this saloon, just this one place you want me out of? What about them other buildings, the one across the street?"

From the other table Tomlain laughed. Billy said quickly, "Oh, you wouldn't be interested in those, Mister Saulter. See," he confided, "this ain't really a town. Not what you'd call a proper one. We've kind of taken it all over. You might call it a company headquarters. So you can see how we wouldn't be interested in having no strangers around."

Saulter nodded slowly. He'd gone as far as he could or would. The rest of it was up to them. "Yes," he said, "I can see that."

"And besides, you're leaving."

"Yes," Saulter said, "I'm leaving." He got up slowly, and went to the bar. Schmidt was standing there, his arms crossed. Saulter nodded at a bottle of the cheap whiskey. "Gimme a bottle of that."

Schmidt set the bottle on the bar. "Dollar and a half."

Saulter took out his shot bag and counted out

six dollars. "And there's another four and a half. That's for me and my horse for three more days." Then, without looking back, he picked up the bottle of whiskey, shouldered his rifle, and walked out of the room. As he left Billy looked over at the other table and shrugged, the gesture saying that he'd done all he could.

Outside, Saulter stood a moment looking around, drawing the clean cold air into his lungs. The sky had turned off a bright blue and the rays from the sun put a sparkling sheen on the snow. But still it was cold, bitterly cold.

Standing there, he looked the other buildings over. Just across what would have been a road if it wasn't hidden by the snow was a large rambling adobe and log building. He could tell it was occupied by the smoke coming out of the chimney. As Saulter looked, a woman suddenly opened the door and came out on the porch. He turned to face her, staring. She looked back. Though she was perhaps fifty yards away he could tell that she was young and fairly good-looking. For a long moment they stood there, staring at each other, her holding the door behind her, him in the snow. Finally, not taking her eyes off him, she backed through the door and disappeared inside. He stood there a moment longer, wondering. It was not a place, nor the country, for such a woman. Seeing her had startled him. This was, he thought, a very strange town. But all he wanted out of it was three days' rest. Then they could have it. He trudged toward the bunkhouse.

Two

SAULTER LAY LIKE a man carefully preserving his strength so that his body could do the job of healing a wound. He lay on his bunk, fully dressed against the cold that swept through the room in spite of the big fireplace at the end. He had the place to himself and the dimming afternoon sunshine made it seem much bigger and bleaker. He lay there, not thinking, not making any plans beyond getting strong enough to travel. He had the big pistol back in his belt; he'd seen to the loading and added an extra cartridge to the safety hole, making it a full six. He didn't plan to stand for any more prodding.

Then the door suddenly banged open, blown out of someone's hand by the wind. Saulter turned his head, tensing. But it was only Schmidt. He came in, banged the door behind him, and stood a moment to stamp the snow off his boots. Then, without preamble, he walked over to Saulter's bunk. "You've got to get out," he said. "Get up and saddle your horse and ride out of here."

With an effort Saulter rolled over and got up on one elbow. He chose his words carefully. "Landlord, I paid for three days for myself and my horse. I intend to stay."

Schmidt had Saulter's money in his hand. He flung it down on the bunk. "Here's your money back. Now get up and leave. Get out of here. I'm throwing you out."

Evenly, Saulter said, "You took the money, Landlord. You can't give it back because they changed your mind for you. This here is a public inn. Pick the money up and put it back in your pocket."

"You've got to go!" Schmidt shouted, stress and worry pitching his voice upward. "I can't have you here. They don't want it!"

Saulter looked at him. "Who are they, Landlord? Who is that crowd, anyway?"

"I don't know!" Schmidt said violently. "And I don't care! But they's five of them and one of you. They're paying good money and been doing it for a considerable spell. They say for you to go. So I'm telling you now I don't have a place for you. Get up!"

Saulter seemed to consider. He drew a long breath that hurt him. "Pick up your money, Schmidt. I'm not leaving. I paid for this bunk and that stall out there and I'm staying. I'm staying for three days and then I'm leaving. I don't want no trouble."

Schmidt suddenly sat down on the next bunk. "Look here," he said, "don't be a fool. That's a rough crowd and they want you to go. I'm not saying," he added guardedly, "but I think it would be a whole lot better for your health if you took their advice. I'm not saying anything, but I can tell you that they mean what they say."

Saulter looked at him mildly. "Why do they want me to go, Landlord? What's going on around here that they need me to leave?"

"I don't know," Schmidt swore violently. "I don't know anything about them. I'm not one of that bunch. They came in here and rented out the town. They're paying good money. It's the best payday I've seen in a long time. I don't ask no questions. I don't concern myself with their business. I just do what they tell me. They tell me you've got to go." He suddenly leaned close to Saulter. "Look here, they're having a hell of an argument. That Tomlain is bad. He wants to deal with you another way. I tell you now, leave. Leave!"

Saulter turned his face away. "Pick your money up, Landlord. I'm staying."

Schmidt looked at him and then shrugged. "You'll leave," he said assuredly, "one way or the other. I give you the advice, but you don't want it. I take my money," he said. He leaned down and scooped up the silver dollars off Saulter's bed. "It won't do you any good where you're going."

Without another word he went out. Saulter sighed and lay back to try and relax.

The afternoon waned. In the saloon the five men were sitting around a table, a bottle of whiskey in front of them. Schmidt had reported back to them that Saulter was not leaving. For the past several hours Tomlain had been working on the hate that had begun when he first laid eyes on Saulter.

"The hell with him," Tomlain said. "I'm gonna put his tail between his legs right now. Or kill him trying."

"Just take it easy, Tomlain," Billy said. "We

don't need none of that. Especially now. You know Mister McGraw don't approve of the way you like to handle things. Just let me ease on over and have another talk with him. Maybe I can make him see the light."

"I'm going to make him see the light," Tomlain growled. "I'm going to fix it so you can see light all the way through him."

"Look here," Billy said, "that won't warsh. And you know it. Mister McGraw is due in here in the next couple of days and he wouldn't be happy about that at all. He said he didn't want us causin' no disturbance. Said he wanted us laying quiet and nice. Killing that pilgrim ain't what he means. What if Saulter's got a half dozen friends looking for him? Or a half dozen enemies. Same difference. We just don't want no company, especially now, not with the job getting this close. I'll talk to him. I still feel like I can make him listen to reason."

"I'll give him reason," Tomlain said. "About six reasons."

Billy sighed. "You don't listen yourself, Tomlain. You know that? Your brains ain't in your head. I just got through explaining, patiently, why we got to be careful now. I'll just talk that old boy into riding on." He gave Tomlain a significant look. "Or would you rather deal with Mister McGraw?"

Tomlain didn't say anything. He looked away from Billy.

"Well? You've already got some explaining to do. You want some more? Or you want to try it my way? Which?"

Tomlain still didn't say anything and Billy prompted him. "Com'on now, answer up. A wink or a nod's the same to a blind mule. You want to handle this, or you want me to? You're mighty quick with that gun, but you ain't too good when it comes to answers. We can do it your way, but you be sure you're ready to explain to Mister McGraw. Well?"

Finally Tomlain pushed back his chair. "Run him off," he answered. "Do it your way." He stood up and started for the bar. But halfway he whirled back around. "But if he don't go I'll tend to it. You understand? And Mister McGraw would say I done right."

Saulter was lying on his bunk. His face was pale and drawn. The door opened and Billy came in, a shaft of sunlight following him. He walked to the bed next to Saulter's and sat down. "Howdy," he said. "Thought I'd come visit."

Saulter nodded.

Billy got out a cigar, licked it, stuck it in his mouth. "Can I light you up one?"

Saulter shook his head.

Billy studied him for a moment. "Neighbor, I've come over here for your best benefit. You're actin' a little more stubborn than is good for you. What say I go ahead and saddle up your horse and help you on out of here? Another town just about ten miles down the road. You could make that easy by tonight."

Saulter smiled slightly. "That's a lie. There's no town near here."

Billy shrugged and grinned. "Just trying to make it easy for you."

Saulter settled himself. "I like it here."

"Now look here, neighbor," Billy said earnestly. "I'm going to have to have a little prayer meeting with your heart. That old dog won't hunt. You've gone and upset Mister Tomlain and he wants you gone. It's took me the better part of an afternoon to talk him out of coming over here and doing something harmful to you. See what I mean? I'm looking out for you and you won't even take my advice."

"I can't leave," Saulter said hoarsely. "I will when I can. In three days."

Billy shook his head. "That just won't do, scout. See, we've got a very important visitor coming in here in the next two days and he wouldn't like you hanging around. I'll tell you at least that much."

Saulter asked, "Why not?"

"Well, let's just say that's his way. Let's just say he don't like strangers around."

"Why not?"

"Mister Saulter, you're getting a little more inquiring than is best for a body's health. Here I'm trying to do you a favor and you won't see it. I told you this ain't really a town. This gentleman in question has bought the place and it's just the same as if you was trespassing. You get my drift? You understand what I mean about trespassing? It's not a healthy occupation. I can understand your problem, what with your wound and all, but I can tell you that if this gentleman sics Mister

Tomlain on you, you'd be a lot better off out on the bald-ass prairie in all this snow."

Billy got up. "I'm going to saddle your horse for you. Then I'm going to come back here and help you gather up your gear and ride on out. It's the sensible thing. And you'll be glad you did it."

"No," Saulter said.

Billy grimaced and threw his cigar down on the floor. "Don't be like that, neighbor. You're into something a little bigger than you want a part of. Look, I'm going the extra mile for you. I'm a southern boy myself, and I can see you're hurt. I comprehend all that. But I'm telling you, you don't know what you're up against." In his earnestness, Billy took off his hat and laid it on the bed. "I'm talking too much, as normal, but I don't really want to see you get killed. Don't see the need. But that's what it's going to come to if you don't get out. I mean that." He stopped and stared at Saulter, waiting for a reaction.

Saulter made none.

"Look here," Billy went on, "just supposing we were wanted men. Just suppose we were on the dodge. Don't you see how it'd be, how we'd feel about company?"

Saulter said, "That ain't it. If you were wanted you wouldn't let me ride out of here."

Billy studied him for a moment. Then he put his hat back on. "You're hardheaded. The way things are it's as easy to kill you as let you go. You keep on makin' push come to shove and the killin' part will get easier. It's your choice." He got up and smiled. "Now I'll go get your horse and you make yourself ready to ride. I'll even stake you to some grub off Schmidt if you're short."

He waited for Saulter to answer, but, when the tall man didn't, wheeled on his heel and went out. Saulter watched him until the door had shut, then with a painful effort, pulled himself up and eased his feet over the side of the bunk. He rested a second, then pulled on his boots, the effort making his face go gray with pain. He got the bottle of whiskey sitting by the side of the bunk, uncorked it, and took a long drink. Then he sat there, his arms resting on his knees, holding the opened bottle loosely in one hand. He didn't want to get up, but he knew he was going to have to. This thing wasn't going to go off by itself so it looked as if he'd have to get up and go handle it. He wished he felt better, stronger. He took another drink of whiskey and corked the bottle and set it back down on the floor.

Just then Billy came back through the door. He came up to the bunk grinning, his face rosy from the cold wind. "Ready to go, scout? Got your horse saddled and tied up outside. Here, let me get your gear." He bent and began to gather up Saulter's bedroll and other belongings. "We ought to get moving. It's getting late and you'll want to make a good camp before dark."

Saulter came slowly to his feet. The weight of the big revolver was a reassuring tug at his waist. He reached for his rifle, but Billy took it. "I'll see to that. I don't imagine you'd go without it." Saulter nodded; he would as soon have both hands free. Billy went on. "Used to have a wife like you and that rifle. Inseparable. Good thing she couldn't shoot as straight as I imagine this piece here does. She caught me being a little too separable one time. Took a real bad attitude about the whole situation." He was talking gaily as he shepherded Saulter toward the door. The tall hunter walked slowly, as if he were pushing a heavy boulder ahead of him.

Billy held the door and they went outside. Saulter looked up. The sky had gone leaden again and little flurries of snow were beginning to fall. His horse was tied just outside. Billy went to the animal and began to load the gear, tying the bedroll on the back and ramming the big rifle home in the boot. "All set," he said, "hop aboard and I'll give you a send-off." He held up a bottle of whiskey he'd taken from his coat. "This is the good stuff. None of the ordinary."

But Saulter walked on by him, toward the saloon. Billy took a step after him. "What's the matter? Where you going?"

"In there," Saulter said, still walking.

Billy came up alongside of him. "Look, you need something? Some grub? I'll get it. You better not go in there."

"No," Saulter said. "I'll tend to it myself." He walked toward the front of the store, his stride becoming more purposeful with every step.

Billy stopped, watching him. "Saulter," he called, "don't do anything foolish."

But Saulter did not answer. He now had his mind on what he must do, though he was not sure yet how he was going to handle it. Unconsciously he reached down and made sure his big coat was unbuttoned so he could get at the Navy Colts.

Then, as he was about to step up on the porch, the door of the house across the street opened. Saulter stopped. The same woman he'd seen earlier came out. She paused, seeing Saulter, and then started down the steps. He watched her. She was wearing a long dress with bunched sleeves. She had a shawl over her head and shoulders and he couldn't see the color of her hair. But he could see, from closer now, that she was prettier than he'd thought before.

She came to the bottom of the steps and stopped. For a long moment there was eye contact between them. Same as before. Some sort of chemistry was passing between them. Then she dropped her eyes and hitched at her shawl. Saulter turned, after one last look, and mounted the steps to the store. He did not pause, but took the doorknob in his right hand and threw it back forcefully.

Inside they looked around as he stood in the doorway. Schmidt was behind the bar, the others were where they'd been, where they never seemed to move from. Carefully Saulter shut the door behind him. He walked slowly to the bar and removed his coat. All the while he kept his eyes fixed on Tomlain.

The gunman said, watching him, "You don't take your coat off when you're leaving, rabbit hunter. Or ain't you smart enough to know that?"

Saulter ignored him, taking the time to put his coat carefully on the bar. He moved down from it just enough so that Schmidt would not be directly behind him. Then he faced the men, speaking pointedly to Tomlain.

"I'm about to get tired of all this bullshit. I don't know what's going on around here and I don't care. But I'm staying a few days and it's going to get goddam dangerous for the next man that saddles my horse for me."

They sat there staring at him for a long second after he'd said that. Then a smile began to spread over Tomlain's face. "Well, well, well," he said softly. Then he got up, moving like a cat after prey he's very sure about. "It's gonna get dangerous all right, snake shooter. But you're the one in the barrel."

He started around the table. Saulter straightened, his hand going to the butt of the gun at his waist. In his mind he was calculating the play. Shoot Tomlain first, of course, but get him with one bullet. Square in the chest. Then there were the two men on Tomlain's left. They might get in each other's way so it would be best to take the one man on the right. But then he didn't know about Billy. He could be at the back door or anywhere. He wasn't worried about Schmidt. He didn't look like the type that was going to involve himself where there was a good chance of getting hurt. Probably he'd go down behind the bar as soon as the guns came out.

Tomlain was still advancing. Saulter watched him with a careful eye. It was dangerous to let him get too close, but there was a point at which he'd be in the line of fire of those behind him and that would give Saulter the extra second he was going to need after he dropped Tomlain. He closed his hand around the butt of his pistol and slid his finger inside the trigger guard. Tomlain had his hand on his own gun and Saulter watched his hand intently, watching for a little tightening that would tell him Tomlain was about to draw.

He calculated one more step and then he was going to kill Tomlain. At that instant the front door opened with a bang. They were all startled. Tomlain stopped and turned; Saulter cautiously turned his head to look. It was the woman, the woman from the house across the street. She stood there in the door, suddenly conscious of the tension in the air, uncertain whether to go or come in.

Saulter broke the strain. Touching his hat brim he said politely, "Miss, I wonder if you'd be good enough to wait outside for just a minute?"

She stared at him searchingly. "What are you talking about?"

"Please, miss," he said. "Just wait outside a moment. Or come back later."

"I will not," she said promptly.

Saulter gestured. "I think it'd be best. Me and these men are about to have some business. I wouldn't want you in the way."

"I've got business here myself," she said, but a look of understanding was coming over her face. She was in her mid-twenties, but there was a hardness about her that made her appear older. She was pretty enough, but in a jaded, determined way. Her face was that of a woman who's seen a lot of the world and who knows there's not much left in it that will either surprise or disappoint her. Or hearten her, for that matter. Seeing the table and understanding what was about to happen, she felt a fleeting bit of sympathy for the tall stranger. Heretofore she'd thought him just to be another gunman that McGraw was importing, but now she could see he was different from the others.

"Please, miss," Saulter said again. There was an appeal in his voice, that of a man who had to get something accomplished while he still had the strength. He touched his hat brim again.

"All right," she said. She gave Saulter a quick look, and then backed out the door. But before she closed it, she called to Schmidt. "Schmidt, we need some more flour. And sugar. And some of those goddam dried apricots. And send us some decent beef."

Schmidt answered, "I'll send Chiffo right over with it, Miss Letty. Right away."

Then she was gone, shutting the door. There was a second of silence, during which the mean smile slowly spread over Tomlain's face again. Looking at him, Saulter thought that he'd have no regret killing such a man. They stood facing, each with a hand on his pistol. Then the back door opened and Billy stepped in. Saulter caught a sidelong glimpse of him out of the corner of his eye. It made it worse, having a man that far off to one side.

And Tomlain was saying, "Now, Mister Big Gun, you were just saying your good-byes." He took another step.

Saulter drew. But, before he could clear his gun, his arms were suddenly pinned from behind by Schmidt. In the confusion of the girl and Billy, he had slipped down the bar until he was right behind Saulter. That, Saulter thought as he struggled, was why Tomlain had been so cocky, so confident.

There was nothing he could do in his weakened condition. Schmidt held him long enough for the other three men to rush up and smother him. They held him by the arms while Tomlain strolled up and planted himself right in front of Saulter. The grin was very big on his face now.

"Now hold on, Tomlain," Billy said. "Just take it easy." He came up behind Tomlain.

Tomlain said to Saulter, "Well, mister man, looks like you've got yourself all fouled in the riggin'. Guess it's about time for you to get that little lesson you've had coming."

"Don't kill him!" Billy said sharply. He put out a hand to stay Tomlain.

The gunman turned and looked at Billy as if he were amazed. "Kill him? Why, I ain't going to kill him! You done told me not to." He turned back to Saulter and licked his lips, enjoying himself. "Course, he may *die*. But I ain't going to kill him."

Without preamble he suddenly hit Saulter in the left side, in the wound, a thudding left and right, bowing his heavy shoulders and driving the blows in with all his strength. Air rushed out of Saulter's lungs in a wailing sigh and all the color went out of his face. He sagged in the arms of the men holding him, passed out from the intense pain.

"There, rabbit trapper. There's a little something for you."

"Goddammit!" Billy swore. He jerked at Tomlain's arm. "You've killed him!"

"Oh, he ain't dead. Are you, snake shooter?" He jerked Saulter's head up by the hair and slapped his face, backhand and forehand.

"Goddammit, leave him alone, Tomlain! You damned animal."

A little color was coming back into Saulter's face. His legs took some of his weight as he tried to straighten.

"Uh, oh," Tomlain said, "look out boys, here he comes again." He let Saulter get fully erect and then timed two jolting left hooks into his damaged side again. Saulter collapsed.

Billy grabbed Tomlain by the arm and slung him back across the room. "Stop it, dammit! Or by god—"

But Tomlain just laughed. "There he is, all ready for you. You can put him on his horse now and send him out of town. He's ready to travel."

At the window the woman's face was evident. She'd been staring in and had seen everything that happened. Now she went toward her house across the street, but stopped to watch as they brought Saulter out of the back of the saloon. He was being supported by two men with Billy leading the way. He was stumbling, his head down, barely able to walk. The men were mostly carrying him. The woman stood near the porch of her building, watching, as they boosted him up on his horse. Billy helped as best he could, to put Saulter's boots in the stirrups. Finally one of the men untied the horse. They passed the reins up and put them in Saulter's nearly nerveless hands.

"Now get out of here!" one of the men yelled. He took off his hat and slapped the horse on the

rump. The animal bolted. Saulter hung on somehow, swaying and sagging weakly in the saddle.
The horse raced past the saloon, wheeled left, and
started out of the town. He went by the woman.
She watched as the horse ran down the road, still
racing under the impetus of the hat slap.

He was quickly out of sight of the men behind
the saloon. One of them walked toward the front
a few yards to make sure that the horse was
heading out of town. "He's gone," he called back.

Billy said, "He's dead for sure."

The other man said, "If Tomlain didn't kill
him, he'll freeze in two hours. But he ought to
make it a few miles first. Won't be found until
spring."

It was starting to snow harder. Billy glanced up
at the flurries of flakes falling. "Let's go in," he
said, "and get a drink. I got a bad taste in my
mouth."

Across the street, Letty stayed to watch. She
was hidden in the darkening shadows of the front
porch and she saw the horse begin to slow as he
hit the edge of town. A little further on and he
came to a stop. Letty could barely make him out;
horse and rider were just a dim blur through the
falling snow. Almost reluctantly she turned the
knob of the front door. "None of my business
anyway," she said under her breath. She swung
the door open. Inside was light and warmth. "Hell
with it," she said again. She went in.

A half mile out of town the horse stood, stamping his feet in the snow, undecided about what to
do. The nearly lifeless Saulter was barely in the

saddle, mostly collapsed on the animal's neck. was only half conscious and aware only of the pain in his chest and side.

It was growing dark, what little daylight there was being obscured by the snow. The horse looked back toward the town. Back there was a warm barn and hay. Out front was nothing but cold. Finally, of his own accord, he turned and took a tentative step back the way he'd come. Then, his head down, trudging because of the unaccustomed load on his neck, the horse made his way slowly back toward the buildings.

In the saloon the men sat around drinking and playing cards. One of them got up and went to the window and peered out. "Good dark," he said. "Sure hate to be in that ol' boy's shoes right now. Ain't even a star to be seen in the sky." He turned from the window and took a chair at the table. Tomlain had the bottle of whiskey at his elbow and the man reached over, took it, and poured himself out a drink. "Quit hogging the whiskey, Tomlain."

The horse came trudging down the street. He walked at a halting pace, uncertain about what to do. Saulter, swaying and slipping in the saddle, was virtually unconscious.

In the house across the street the woman was watching out the window of the front room. The room was rough and crudely furnished; behind her were several other women who looked, in makeup and type, very much like her. They watched her.

One of them said, "What the hell are you doing, Letty? Have you gone crazy from all this damn snow?"

"Shut up," she said without looking around. But she herself didn't know why she was keeping the vigil. Then she thought she saw something, a movement, a shape, in the black night. She went to the door and stepped out on the front porch. Saulter and his horse were standing in the middle of the road, nearer to her house than the saloon.

From behind her one of the women called, "Letty, shut that damned door!"

"Shut up," she said automatically, her eyes on Saulter. But she pulled the door to behind her, undecided about what to do with this problem in the road. But even as she watched, Saulter slowly slid down the side of the horse and fell in the snow. For a second he lay there. The motion had startled the horse, but Saulter still had the reins clutched in his hands. The coldness of the snow seemed to revive him for an instant. He tried to rise, agony in every movement. He almost got to his knees, then he pitched forward and lay face-down, motionless.

Letty looked quickly toward the saloon. The lighted windows were dim and empty and she could see there was no one outside.

At the card table Tomlain was ragging Billy. "When you goin' into nursin'? I think you'd look mighty good in one of them outfits they wear."

Billy let him talk, watching him over the rim of his glass of whiskey.

"Now you understand I didn't kill him," said

Tomlain. He laughed at his own joke. "And you can't tell Mister McGraw I brought us no trouble by killing him. Now can you? Can you?"

Billy suddenly got up and walked to the bar. "Tomlain," he said, "I've done a bunch of sorry business in my time. And I'll do more because I'm cheap enough to sell myself for a dollar." He turned to face the gunman. "But you're just trash."

Letty stood there on the porch staring at Saulter spread-eagled in the snow. She had folded her arms and pulled the shawl tighter around her as protection against the biting snow, but she hadn't moved. Saulter just lay there, the snow already threatening to cover him. The horse stood patiently by, now and again stamping a hoof.

The door behind her opened and one of the other women came out. "What are you doing out in this—" Then she saw Saulter. "Oh, God," she exclaimed. "Is that the one?"

"Go back in," Letty told her tersely.

"Now, Letty," the woman warned. "Don't be thinking of doing anything about him. Ain't none of our affair."

"Get inside!" Letty ordered. "I mean it, goddammit!"

"Letty, McGraw is coming," the woman said. But she opened the door to go back in the house. Letty suddenly turned and called through the opening. "Juno! Juno! Come here!" She told the woman, "Get in there and send Juno out here."

The woman went in and closed the door while Letty carefully descended the steps and walked over to Saulter. For a moment she stared down at him, then she knelt and tentatively touched his back as if assuring herself it was a man lying there. She started to turn him over, looked back toward the house, started to yell, "Juno!" then broke off in mid-syllable and glanced quickly toward the saloon. She got up and went back to the house and stepped inside.

The maid, Juno, was at the window with the other women. Before Letty could say anything, one of the women came forward. "Listen," she said determinedly, "you better not get mixed up in this. You better leave that man alone."

"Shut up," Letty told her. She motioned to her maid. "Juno, didn't you hear me call you? Come along. I want you to help me."

But the other woman said, "Listen, you're not bringing him in here. You're not getting the rest of us mixed up in this. I mean it."

Letty turned on her furiously. "Shut up, Hester, you damn bitch. Go to your room. If you don't want any part of this, go up and cover your eyes. But shut up!"

She went out with the Spanish maid following her. The cold hit them like a physical force. The maid shivered and complained, but Letty ignored it. She knelt by Saulter and, with Juno's help, turned him over. His breathing was hoarse and ragged. She bent and listened to his chest. "He's alive," she said, "but not much else. We got to get him in the house. Help me get him on his feet."

Juno seemed afraid to touch him. "Get his shoulder, dammit!" Letty said sharply. "He won't bite you."

Together and with much effort, they slowly raised him first to his knees and then to his feet. His eyes fluttered open and he coughed. "What?" he said hoarsely.

"It's all right," Letty told him. "Just hold on to us. We're taking you in the house."

They supported him up the steps into the house, a big arm over each of their shoulders. He seemed to go in and out of consciousness. Sometimes he would be almost walking under his own power and then he would sag down and it would be all the two women could do to hold him up.

They got him through the front door. The other women were standing around, openmouthed. "Goddammit," Letty swore at them. "Help me. Help me get him up the stairs. We'll put him in Juno's room. They'd never go in there."

They would not have made it, jammed in the tight stairwell, if he hadn't come to long enough to help them at the last. They eased him through the doorway of a tiny room and then down on the bed. He said haltingly, "My horse."

"Don't worry," Letty told him. "We'll see to it."

They got him in the bed and then Letty took Juno to the stairs and told her to put Saulter's horse in the barn. Then she stopped her. "No," she said, "wait a minute." She thought. "They'd find him. Just—just get that big rifle of his and his saddlebags. Leave the horse. They'll think he fell off and the horse came back." She went back in the room to see to Saulter.

Across the street the men were playing cards. Tomlain looked over toward the window and laughed. "I bet that big hunter could use a drink right now. Bet he's a little cold."

Billy looked at him. "Shut up and play, Tomlain. You calling the bet or not?"

"Always," Tomlain said. He laughed again. "I always call, Billy boy. You remember that."

None of them saw Juno as she scurried out of the house, quickly took Saulter's gun and saddlebags, and then raced back into the warmth.

THREE

THE MORNING OPENED quiet and clear. In the bunkhouse Tomlain and Billy and the other three men stirred themselves awake and gathered in front of the fireplace where Chiffo had laid on a good blaze. Billy and one of the other gunmen were dressed, but the others were still in their long underwear though they'd pulled on boots and hats. They stood sulkily, listlessly, some of them feeling the effects of too much whiskey the night before, warming themselves from the cold.

Tomlain growled. "Where's that goddam Indian with the coffee?"

At that instant the door of the bunkhouse opened and Chiffo stumbled over the sill bearing a huge coffeepot and a handful of tin cups. He tried unsuccessfully to kick the door to first, and then to edge it back with his body, but it was unwieldy and wouldn't budge. Finally, Tomlain yelled, "Shut that Eskimo hole, you heathen bastard! And get that coffee up here damn quick or I'll kick your tail up between your shoulder blades."

Chiffo scurried in, stopped, and looked bewildered.

"Put the coffeepot down and shut the door," Billy called. "Then bring the coffee up here to the fire."

The boy gave Billy a grateful look, did as he was

told, and then finally came forward with the
coffee. Tomlain jerked the pot out of his hand
before he could set it down, poured himself a cup,
and handed the pot around. Chiffo stood by, a
hopeful, anxious smile on his face. "You buy me
a little wheesky now, maybe?"

Tomlain suddenly whirled, spilling his coffee,
and swung a kick at the boy. "Get your ass out of
here or I'll buy you something all right!" he
yelled.

Chiffo jumped back out of the way and then ran
for the door. When he was gone the men stood
around drinking coffee and scratching and yawning. Gradually they began dressing piece by piece,
gaining energy as the coffee took hold.

Finally one of them asked, "Reckon Mister
McGraw will get in today?"

"Ought to be real soon," Billy said. He gave
Tomlain a significant look. "Judging by what that
pilgrim said about them railroads gettin' close to
tiein' in to each other."

Another tall, thin man they called Barney
spoke up. "You know, that just confounds hell out
of me how they can do that—join them tracks up
like that. I understand they started one out from
the east coast and the other'n from the west coast
and they *plan* to meet head-on somewhere out in
the slam middle of the country!"

"In Utah," Billy said. "Right about fifty miles
north of here."

"Well, hell and damnation," Barney exclaimed,
"how do they find one another? I've rid back and
forth across that country and it's mighty wide and
lonesome. I've been lost with just me and my

horse, never mind about draggin' no railroad along behind."

"They survey," Billy explained. "They got surveyors out."

"A surveyor? What the hell's that?"

"Oh, shut your face," Tomlain growled irritably.

"Well, I just can't understand it. Them comin' all that way and then dabbin' into each other."

"What the hell you care?" Tomlain asked him angrily. "What the hell you care how they do it? Your job don't start till they do it. After that is when you earn your money. And damn good money it is, so just shut up and let me drink this coffee."

They fell silent again, just the sound of slurping coffee breaking the quiet of the long room. Then Billy turned slowly to Tomlain. "This is some deal, ain't it? I shore never figured I'd be in on something this big."

"It's big," Tomlain agreed. He licked his lips.

Billy hunched forward. He started to speak, hesitated, and then said, "I wonder . . . I mean, I wonder if it ain't maybe a little too big."

"How's that?" Tomlain asked him. He unbuttoned his undershirt and scratched his chest, the black hair matted so heavy it looked like black fur.

"Well . . . think about it. I mean, this is kinda serious. You ain't worried about it? Maybe even a little scared?"

Tomlain gave him a cold glance. "I ain't scairt of nothing, boy."

Billy gave a sour look. "Oh, come off it, Tomlain. I'm talking straight now, not saloon talk. It ain't like we was going in to rob a bank or kill an ordinary citizen. You talking about the power. Any man that's got any sense has got to be a little nervous about such doings."

"He's just a target to me," Tomlain said contemptuously. "He'll bleed same as a stuck hog."

Barney was unable to keep quiet any longer. He'd been listening to the talk eagerly. Now he put in, "Yeah, and that's another thing's got me dumbfounded. Why, look at all this power of fuss we're going to just for the sake of one man. Why, they'll be nine of us all told. And just a world of plannin' and the money bein' spent."

"He ain't exactly an ordinary citizen," Billy said gently. "You don't just walk up and stick a pistol in his belly."

"Well, is they guards and all like that around? Troopers and such?"

"Shut up, goddammit!" Tomlain said violently. "Can't you keep that trap of yours closed for five seconds?"

Barney looked grieved. "Well, I can't help wondering, can I? Here Mister McGraw has gathered up the finest set of gunmen and desperadoes in the country. Men that know how to get a job done no matter what it—"

"Aw, lay off it," Billy said. "Sometimes you talk too much. Job like this, it's better just to do it and not worry it to death."

They had finally all dressed and one man walked by shrugging into his coat. "Guess I'll look at the weather," he said to no one in particular. He went out the end door of the bunkhouse, shutting it carefully behind him. For a moment he stood there yawning and stretching in the dazzling whiteness of the morning. Finally he looked toward Schmidt's. He saw a horse standing there, just to the leeward side, his reins hanging abandoned. The man took a step or two closer, looking hard at the horse. Then he suddenly whirled and raced back in the bunkhouse. "Hey, Tomlain," he yelled, jerking his thumb. "You better come here an' look. I think that hunter is back."

Tomlain was sitting on a bunk, still drinking coffee. He turned slowly to look at the man. "What?" he asked flatly.

"That goddam hunter's horse is out there. Right behind Schmidt's."

Without another word Tomlain got up, found his gunbelt, put it on, and then led the others as they trooped through the door. As they went he spoke to Billy, "If that sonofabitch is back we'll see who's head it's on now. Wouldn't let me kill him. Well, we'll see what Mister McGraw says."

They trudged through the snow, staring hard at the horse as they came. The animal, looking drawn and sorry from his long night in the freezing weather turned his head and stared back. They ranged up along his side and Billy went to his head and took up the reins. "Hell," he said, "this horse came back in here on his own. Look at that." He pointed to the heavy crust of snow on the saddle. "He's been standing out here all night. And these reins are just hanging loose. Nobody rode this horse in here. He wandered in."

"By the lord," Barney said, "I do believe you be right."

Tomlain looked at the horse and then the snow around him. He licked his lips. "I don't know," he said.

"Sure," Billy said, "it's plain as paint." He pointed. "Horse is still saddled, but the saddlebags and that old boy's rifle are gone. He got off that horse somewhere up the line to try and make him a camp. Probably weak as skimmed milk. He got his rifle and his saddlebags off and then the horse got away from him. Maybe he even collapsed."

"I don't know," Tomlain said again. He rubbed his black-whiskered jaw. "Could be."

"Looks likely," one of the other men said. "Horse ain't dumb. He wadn't gonna stand out in that cold and freeze. He made back for the only place he knew where they was a barn and hay."

"Maybe so," Tomlain said again.

"Hell," Billy insisted. "Ain't no maybe about it. That man is laying up the line somewhere makin' a hump under the snow."

Instinctively they all walked to the front of Schmidt's and looked up the road. It was all snow as far as they could see. Nothing to break the whiteness. "Nothing could live out in that," Billy said. "Not no man on foot and hurt."

"We still ought to look around a little," Tomlain said. "Make sure he didn't ride back in and hole up."

"That can't hurt nothin'," Billy agreed. "Well, we know he ain't in the bunkhouse or Schmidt's or the women's house. That just leaves the barns and them two other buildings over yonder. Barney, you take that horse and put him up in the barn back of the women's place. They got more room and they ain't no point in lettin' a good animal stand out here and freeze. Then have a look around while the rest of us look them other buildings over."

At an upstairs front window of the women's house, a girl looked out at the men beginning to disperse for the search. She watched for a moment and then turned away. The room was still dim, the morning's sun not having fully illuminated it yet. Letty was lying in one chair, asleep, and Juno in another. Saulter was lying on the bed, also asleep. He stirred restless from time to time with the pain. The girl at the window went over to Letty and shook her by the shoulder. "Letty . . . Letty . . ."

Letty came awake with a start. She looked first at the girl and then across at Saulter. She straightened in the chair and yawned. "Goddammit, Brenda, don't startle me like that."

"Tomlain and that bunch have come out and seen his horse." She gestured to Saulter. "They look like they fixin' to search."

Letty got up and went to the window, but the men had disappeared by then. "They won't come in here," she said with assurance.

"Wonder what they'll think?" the girl asked.

"What the hell do I care what they think," Letty answered irritably. "They'll think what they ought to think. That he fell off his horse and froze and the horse came back here."

"What if they don't?" Brenda was a young, pretty, slightly dumb-looking girl. "Why, they're terribly bad. No telling what they'd do to us if they knew that man was here."

Letty was gruff from having awakened from a nearly sleepless night. "Why should they think he's here? This is the last place they'd look. And they wouldn't come in Juno's room. They ain't gonna think a bunch of whores would take a man in off the street like that."

"Well, why did we take him in? I don't really understand that."

Letty frowned at her for a moment, then shrugged and half smiled. "Maybe I ain't a whore at heart. Who knows? What the hell difference does it make? So long as everybody keeps their mouth shut we ain't got any worry."

"Oh, I ain't gonna say anything, Letty," Brenda promised. "You don't have to worry about that." She stole a glance over at Saulter. "My goodness, he is kind of good-lookin', ain't he? So handsome and genteel and all."

"Looks like a man," Letty said grimly. She walked over to Saulter's bed. "And I've seen enough of them in my lifetime to last me through all my years in hell."

"Then I still don't understand," Brenda began. But Letty cut her off with, "Oh, shut up about it, Brenda. There's lots you don't understand." She put her hand on Saulter's brow. "Wake Juno up and let's have a look at him now he's lasted the night. One of ya'll fetch some hot water and clean cloths and some scissors."

• • •

Across the street, Tomlain and the others had gathered on the front porch of Schmidt's. They stood around, looking off in the distance and smoking.

"Well, he might'a come back in on that horse last night," Barney said, "but he left again on foot cause he ain't in this here town. Nowhere."

"Maybe," said Tomlain.

Billy made a disgusted sound. "No maybe about it. The man is laying out yonder froze like an icicle."

"Maybe," Tomlain said, "somebody ought to ride out the road and see if they's any sign of him."

"Under two foot of snow?" Billy asked. "It *snowed* all night, Tomlain. What you want to do, dig up every mound?"

"I don't know," Tomlain answered slowly. He rubbed his jaw. "With McGraw due in I don't want no slipups. I'd like to be sure."

"What's the matter, Tomlain? Think you're slipping? Them licks you gave that man I'm surprised he didn't die on the spot. You figure he was still in shape to take off cross-country? Didn't it fall out just about the way you'd figured?"

Tomlain smiled slowly and licked his lips. "Well," he said, "I guess that's right."

Billy said, "I never seen you worry over some old boy like you've done over that hunter. Did you figure he was more than you could handle?"

Tomlain gave him a look. "I figure he got handled. I figure they'll find him the first spring thaw. Just like I planned it." He turned and spit. "Hell with it. Let's get a drink."

In Juno's room Letty was bending over Saulter. She had opened his shirt and cut his undershirt away. The exposed bandage was soaked and crusted with old blood. She began cutting it away with the scissors. "Damn fool men," she muttered under her breath.

Juno and Brenda were by her side and the other three women were crowded in just at the door. They all looked like Letty: half-pretty, young women, fancily dressed in a cheap way, but hardened long before their time by their profession. They watched intently, not unkindly, but with an apprehension about Saulter's presence. "Goddammit," Letty said over her shoulder, "don't all you stand there gawking. One of you go down to the parlor. One of them fools from across the street is liable to get the urge even this early in the morning and I wouldn't want them wandering around the house looking for company." Nobody moved. "Go on, goddammit!" Letty said angrily. She glared until one of the girls disengaged herself unwillingly and went down the stairs.

Letty cut the bandage through in two places and then tugged it loose with an effort. It came off hard, stuck to Saulter by the dried blood. He was still asleep or unconscious, but he stirred restlessly with the pain.

"Oh, it's hurtin' him!" Brenda said.

Letty paid her no attention, just went on stripping off the bandage. When she'd exposed the wound all the other women gasped. It was ugly.

The bullet wound itself would not have been too serious. It was far enough to the side to have missed his vital organs. But the flesh around it was massively bruised and purple and the skin was shriveled and sick looking. The bullet hole was clean, with ragged edges that would have healed themselves.

Letty shook her head. "Ain't that a mess," she said disgustedly. "Fool got himself shot and then that Ray Tomlain give him a little fist doctoring. Wonder he's alive." She felt around the wound with tender fingers. Saulter groaned and thrashed. "Broken ribs in there, but there's nothing we can do about that. Let's get it cleaned up. Juno, get me that hot water and some lye soap. Then I want some of that rotgut whiskey to pour in the wound. That ought to finish him off. Then we got to turn him over and get at it from the back. So I'll need some help."

Brenda pointed at the gunshot hole. "Wonder how he came by that?"

"Oh, shut up, Brenda. Men don't need no reason to do things like this to one another. If they ain't a reason they'll think of one or else do it out of meanness." She began to probe around the wound, feeling the extent of the ribs Tomlain had broken.

As she worked, Saulter stirred in pain. His eyelids flickered a little, but they didn't open. Somewhere inside his head his mind was working and he was remembering, remembering the same feeling of pain when he'd got the wound.

It was a big saloon tent, the kind you'd find in a forward line camp of a railroad that was laying transcontinental track. It was like the many others scattered around the work site at the rail head. There were other saloon tents, a few cook tents, and one whorehouse under canvas. They were there because the men who were building the railroad knew that you couldn't take men out across a desolate wilderness and work them in satisfaction without fulfilling basic needs that they had besides food and water. The tents moved as the work did, never staying so far behind that a man couldn't easily reach them from the dormitory cars. During the day they were mostly slow, quiet enough so that you could hear the distant ring of iron hammers driving iron spikes to nail the rails together. But then at night, after the men had cleaned up and had supper, they were smoky noisy hells where the rules were what you might expect.

Saulter wasn't often found in the tents for he was mostly out on a meat hunt. But when he was in camp he would sometimes drop in for a drink or a game of cards. Not that he mixed much. He wasn't a man who had many intimates.

The tent he entered that night was smoky and dim from the poorly trimmed kerosene lanterns. There was a makeshift bar, a number of rickety tables, and a large crowd. Most of them were railroad workers, tired after a hard day's work. But mixed in were a few hard-looking dance hall women and the inevitable gamblers. There was a poker layout, a roulette table, and several faro layouts.

Saulter made his way easily through the

crowd, not having to push or shove for the men, turning and recognizing him, made way instinctively. He was wearing his heavy coat and carrying his big rifle and you could see, from the dried blood on the front of his deerskin leggings, that he'd just returned from a hunt. He nodded briefly to one or two men and went to the bar and ordered whiskey. Two men at a faro table in a back corner were watching him intently. They had no players at their table though the other games did, and the dealer sat flipping the top of his faro box up and down idly. When they saw Saulter they whispered together briefly for a moment and then the man sitting across from the dealer, who was his confederate, his shill, leaned back in his chair and called to the hunter. "Hey, Saulter!" he yelled over the noise. "Saulter! Over here, Saulter."

Saulter took a long moment acknowledging the call. Finally he turned his head toward the corner and looked at the man. He didn't say anything.

"Hey, Saulter! Com'on over. Com'on over and play." They were only twenty feet apart, but the noise and the crush were such that it was difficult to hear.

Saulter looked at the man, then his eyes shifted to the dealer behind the table.

"Aw, com'on," the man yelled. "Jack here's running cold. We can take him easy. Com'on and let's get a game started."

"No," Saulter said. He turned around now and faced the men because he had sensed something, had sensed it as soon as the man first called to him. He expected there would be trouble of some kind, he just didn't know how far it was going to go.

"Let him go, Charlie," said Jack, the dealer. "Can't you see Mister Saulter doesn't want to play?"

But Charlie was insistent. "Aw, com'on, Saulter. Com'on and play."

Saulter didn't respond, nor did he take his eyes off the dealer.

"No, Charlie, that ain't the way." The dealer smiled sarcastically. "Don't you know Mister Saulter is a fine southern gentleman? You don't want to be yellin' at him like that. Take him a handwritten invitation on a lace doily. That's what *Mister* Saulter expects."

It was as if someone had held up a hand to the crowd to quiet them. Men near the confrontation heard the words and stopped talking and then others further away caught the sense and they too became quiet.

Jack went on. "But, Mister Saulter, how come you come in a nice place like this in them stinking clothes covered with stinking buffalo blood? Ain't you got no manners, Mister Saulter?"

Saulter said, slowly, "You kill buffalo for meat and you're going to get some blood on you. But it's a lot harder on the buffalo."

The shill put in, "Aw now, com'on, let's be friends. Com'on now and play, Saulter."

"Let it be, Charlie," Jack said evenly. "Mister Saulter has opinions about the way I deal this game. Opinions he hasn't kept to himself." He was still playing with the faro case, raising and lowering the lid with one hand while his other hand was out of sight behind the box.

"Now see," Charlie said earnestly, "there it is right there, Saulter. See how these misunderstandings get started? See, folks won't play in Jack's game because they think you've been going around saying he runs a crooked game. And you know that ain't so. And folks pay such a considerable attention to what you say that you've got to be extra careful. That's just the way these little misunderstandings get started. So why don't you come on over and play and let everybody see that's what it is, a little misunderstanding. Come take a hand or two and that'll clear the whole mess up."

Saulter didn't bother to speak.

Charlie went on, insisting, "You never said old Jack run a crooked game, now did you, Saulter?"

Saulter looked at him a long moment. "No," he finally said.

Charlie looked around triumphantly. "See? See there, folks? You heard it yourself."

But Saulter continued. "I said he cheated."

It somehow got even quieter in the place. The dealer stopped flipping the box lid. "You calling me a chat?" His voice was dangerous.

"No," Saulter answered easily, "I can't call you a cheat because I'm not around you at all times. All I can say is that every time I've seen you deal you've cheated."

"Then you're calling me a cheat."

Saulter shrugged. He had expected this when the man, Charlie, had first called to him, had indeed expected it for some time. It could only end one way. He said slowly, "Have it your own way."

At the words the gambler suddenly flipped the faro case aside. He was holding a pistol behind it, the barrel pointed straight at Saulter. There was an instant, as his finger tightened on the trigger, that gave Saulter a chance to flinch to his side. It wasn't much, but it kept the bullet from taking him square. He had his own pistol drawn, drawing even as he moved, but the gambler fired first, the gun making a huge roar against the canvas walls. The force of the bullet knocked Saulter back against the bar and down to one knee. Grimacing at the pain he thumbed off a shot that took the gambler full in the chest. He went over backwards in his chair, disappearing underneath the table. Then Saulter was swinging to the left. The shill had his pistol out and was aiming. But Saulter fired first. The first bullet took the man in the shoulder, spinning him around, the second caught him in the left chest and he went down in a heap. For a second, in the sudden quiet, Saulter peered through the blue smoke. Then, grimacing, he put his hand to his ribs and looked at the blood that came off his palm. Slowly he went down to one knee, his head tilted back, his eyes shut.

They had him in the hospital tent, lying on a cot. Someone had taken off his coat and shirt and a doctor was finishing bandaging his chest and sides. A man in whipcord riding pants and boots and a Stetson hat was standing at the foot of the bed. He nodded when Saulter opened his eyes. "How you feel?"

Saulter grunted, letting his body gingerly feel itself out. "All right," he answered.

"Doc here says it ain't too bad. Didn't hit your lungs or nothing vital. Just going to be sore as hell for a while. Ripped out some of your white meat and you lost a good bit of blood."

Saulter didn't smile.

The doctor went on working. In a moment he was through. He stepped back and told the man in the whipcord breeches, "He'll be all right in a few days. All he really needs is rest. He's got a hole in him that needs to plug itself up."

"Thanks," the man said. He waited until the doctor had departed and then came around and sat down on the cot next to Saulter's. He looked at the hunter intently. "I got a bad piece of business to do and I'd just as soon get it over with. Do you feel well enough?"

Saulter nodded slowly, his eyes on the man's face.

"I don't like what I've got to do, but it's got to be. I've got my orders and I've got a railroad to run. Now you're the best hunter I've ever seen and it was a fair fight, but the fact is I've got to let you go. You've got to clear out of here. Stay a couple of nights and then I want you gone."

Saulter slowly raised his head off the pillow and cocked his head at the man.

"Goddammit," the foreman said. "Don't look at me like that. I know what a lousy sonofabitchin' deal it sounds like, but look at it from my side. I don't make the rules but I got to carry 'em out. There's always been a rule about trouble in camp. All parties, right or wrong, have to clear out. But it's worse than that. We're nearing completion and I just can't risk any trouble whatsoever. I know those two needed killing. Yes, and they asked for it. But they'll have friends, their kind always does. And there'll be more trouble. You know it as well as I do. I just can't risk it, Saulter. Not now."

Saulter said distinctly, "Shit."

The foreman nodded. "I agree." He got up and began striding up and down. "Look, I know a few things you don't know. We got about thirty more miles of track to lay and then this show is going to be over anyway. So there wasn't much job left as it was. But right soon I'm going to have some high mucky-muck government offi-cials around my neck and I can't have no trouble. Of any kind."

Saulter let his head back down on the pillow. "Don't strain yourself to explain," he said.

"Damn you, Saulter," the man said. He stopped his pacing. "Don't come that on me. We've been friends and I'm giving you this straight."

"Thanks," Saulter said dryly.

"Look here. I tell you, this ain't no ordinary time. When I say high mucky-muck govern-ment officials, I mean high! Some of the high-est. If you knew what I know you wouldn't be so goddam quick to condemn me. I'd like to tell you just exactly who may be arrivin' down to drive that last spike. But I can't. Just take my word for it that there's no way I can risk any trouble." He stopped, waiting for Saulter to speak. Saulter said nothing.

"Don't make it no easier on me, Saulter," the foreman said disgustedly. "Well, you're trouble any way you look at you. Men see you and they've just got to try you, got to find out. By the time they understand they've made a mistake it's too late and I've got another body on my hands. Well, I don't blame you. You're the way you are and you've got a right to be that way. And you can back it up. But trouble follows you and I can't take no chances. So you've got to get out. Now I'll see that you draw a month's wages. Hell, make it two months'. And you leave with my best wishes and references. Not that you could give a damn about that. But that's how it is."

Saulter deliberately closed his eyes.

"Suit yourself," the foreman said. He turned for the door. "Good luck, Saulter."

Saulter waited until he was gone and then he slowly sat up. He took a long moment drawing deep breaths. Finally, when he felt like he could stand the pain, he swung his legs around to the floor. With painful movements he dressed himself and then got up and put on his hat and shrugged into his coat. Lastly he picked up his big rifle. He walked out the door, favoring his left side. Outside it was starting to snow slightly.

Four

SAULTER'S EYES FLICKERED open as Letty finished bandaging him. He jumped slightly, then raised his head for a quick look around the room. "Oh, don't get jumpy," Letty said. "You're all right."

"What?" he asked, the single word encompassing his whole situation and how he got there.

She understood. "Never mind now, I'll tell you all about it later." When she spoke to Saulter there was a perceptible softening of her tone.

As if she'd been waiting for Saulter to wake so he too could hear what she had to say, one of the girls at the door, a hard-faced woman of twenty-five, spoke up. "Listen, Letty," she said, "I don't like this one little bit. What business is this of ours? We want him out of here."

"Oh, shut up, Hester," Letty told her.

"Listen, I mean it. You want to get us all killed? That bunch over there finds him in here and that Tomlain just as soon beat you to death as look at you. We've been talking about it all night and you've got no right to do this."

Letty turned on her in a blazing fury. "Listen, you little bitch, don't you tell me what to do! I'm still running this house. All of you, just keep your mouths shut and they'll never know a thing. We can hide him here. He needs a few days' rest and he's by god going to get it! You hear me!"

The women at the door wilted before her. She

took a step toward Hester. "And you better make sure everybody stays shut up, Hester, because if you don't I'll tell them *you* brought him in here. And they'll believe me. McGraw especially. You got that?"

Hester said, "Now, Letty . . . Now, Letty . . ."

"Go on," Letty ordered. "Get out of here. All of you."

She shooed them out and then stood by his bed, watching as they disappeared. Finally she looked down at him. "You're all right," she said. "The wound's not bad. You're just exhausted and need some food and to get your strength back." She started away, but his hand suddenly darted out and caught her wrist. She looked down and their eyes locked. He said, "I don't want to cause you any trouble . . . Letty." He hesitated over the name.

"Don't worry."

He continued holding her wrist. Finally she bent down and kissed him gently on the lips. Then she straightened up. "You sleep. You'll be all right here. I'm going down and fix you some barley soup with beef in it. Go to sleep." She went out the door, closing it behind her. For a second he stared after her. Then his eyes went to the bed and his surroundings. He brought his hand up and fingered the faded lace of the quilt that covered him. Finally his gaze wandered over to the corner where his big rifle stood. His revolver and other belongings were piled around it. Then he seemed to relax. He closed his eyes and went to sleep.

• • •

The short winter day waned. Occasionally Letty looked in, but he continued to sleep. Once she sent Juno up with a bowl of broth which the maid spoon-fed to Saulter. When he'd finished he let his head drop back down on the pillow. "Where's Letty?" he asked. "She busy," Juno told him. He nodded slightly and then closed his eyes and went back to sleep.

Downstairs, in what served as the parlor in the rough building, the girls were lounging around in various stages of boredom and undress. Letty came in the room and looked grimly around for a moment. "All right, sisters," she said sharply. "It's open house tonight. Time to start getting up and getting ready. Your gentlemen callers will be here soon. Move, dammit!"

They got up lethargically and began going to their rooms. Letty looked around, then took her shawl and stepped out on the front porch. First she looked across at the saloon. Then she looked off in the distance, north toward where the snow-filled road wound. Dark was coming fast. As she stood there, Barney came out on the porch and called across to her, "Hey, Letty, all right for us to come on now?"

"Not yet," she said. She turned to go, then turned back and yelled across to Barney. "And goddammit, ya'll had better be shaved and you better be clean!"

"Aw, Letty," he answered.

"I mean it!" she insisted. "Anybody comes over here smelling like a pig they ain't going to get in." With that she turned and entered the house.

Saulter lay in the darkened room. He appeared asleep, but as the door opened, his eyes flashed and his hand instinctively came out from under the covers with his pistol. Then he saw it was Letty and he lowered the gun and smiled. She was carrying a bowl of broth. Steam rose from it in the chill of the room.

"How you feel?" she asked.

"Better," he said. "What time is it? Morning or night?"

"Night," she said. "You've slept all day." She sat down on the side of the bed by him and started to feed him the broth. But he turned his head slightly.

"Wait," he said, "I want to find out a few things."

"Not now," she answered briskly, and insisted with the spoon to his mouth. "I haven't got time. I want you to eat this and I've got to hurry."

She forced the food on him, cramming the spoon rapidly in his mouth. He protested. "It's hot!"

"That's all right," she said, "you're tough."

"Stop," he commanded. He took the bowl out of her hand, set it on his chest, and took the spoon. "I can feed myself."

"All right. But you be sure you eat it all." She stood up. "I've got to go and get dressed. Listen, they're coming over tonight. You stay awake if you can. I'm going to lock this door, but if some of them should insist on coming in you've got to make it into that wardrobe." She indicated a big clothes chest standing against the wall. As if to illustrate, she gathered up his gear, swung back the door of the chest, and crammed his stuff inside. "Do you think you could make it over here if you had to?"

"Yes," he said, looking at her.

She went back over to him. "Let me look at you." She took up the bowl of soup and swept back the cover with one hand and studied the bandage. Just a trace of blood had seeped through. "Looks all right. Not too tight, is it?"

"No," he said, his eyes holding at her face.

"I've got to go," she said. But once again he caught her wrist. For a long second he looked in her eyes.

"Will you be with them?" He jerked his head toward the window.

"What the hell you think my job is?" she asked harshly. Then she jerked her hand free and went out the door, shutting it behind her. Saulter heard the sound of a key turning.

It grew late. Downstairs, they were well warmed up. Barney was playing a harmonica and Billy was dancing with one of the girls to *Buffalo Gal, Won't You Come Out Tonight?* The two other killers were kissing and mauling two of the other girls. Only Tomlain was aloof. He sat in a chair, drinking straight out of a bottle of whiskey and glowering across at Letty, who was sitting alone in a chair. She was elegantly, though gaudily, dressed yet she didn't really seem to be a part of the scene. The men whooped and hollered and drank whiskey and the girls laughed and giggled. Occasionally one of the men slipped off into a side room with a girl.

Upstairs, Saulter lay in the semi-darkness, his eyes open, listening intently. He had his pistol out on top of the cover and he idly cocked and uncocked it, being careful to let the hammer down gently with his thumb. The sounds of the party came distinctly, if distantly, into his room.

Downstairs the party had grown louder and wilder and more drunken. Tomlain was still sitting across the room from Letty. Only now he was scowling, his face flushed from all the whiskey. He seemed to be working himself up to a pitch of some kind. All of a sudden he heaved himself up and made his way determinedly across to Letty. She barely glanced up, but he reached down and grabbed her wrist. "Com'on," he growled, "me an' you is goin' to the room."

She twisted her arm violently, trying to free herself. "Let me go, you big ape. Goddammit!"

He hauled her to her feet. "Miss high and mighty. Let's see how you like what I'm going to give you." He started to drag her away, but she pulled back and then fetched him a tremendous slap in the face. It so startled him that he dropped her wrist. "You sonofabitch!" she told him, her eyes spitting fire. "Don't you ever touch me again."

"Goddam you!" Tomlain roared. He pulled back to hit her, but Billy caught his arm.

"Hold on, Tomlain," Billy said. "McGraw won't like this."

"You goddam right McGraw won't like it," Letty spit. "You touch me again and McGraw will like it even less."

Tomlain lowered his fist, but he was no less

angry. "McGraw's special piece. You think that makes you untouchable?"

"It does where you're concerned," she said.

"You're a whore, ain't you?" Tomlain sneered at her.

"Sure," she answered, "I'm a whore. By profession. But you're a whore by nature."

Tomlain's face clammed, but Billy turned him around. "Com'on, Ray. Com'on and sit down and let's drink some whiskey. Sheila, come over here and keep old Tom company."

Letty glared after them, then finally sat back down. The party started up again, but it had lost its spark.

Upstairs, Saulter lay staring straight ahead, his eyes wide open, his thumb rapidly cocking and uncocking the revolver. Tomlain's loud voice had carried clearly to his ears.

It grew later. Letty remained in her chair while the party slowly died around her. Barney was asleep on the floor. Tomlain lay tipped back in his chair, his head on his chest, a bottle of whiskey hanging loosely from his hand. Billy was laying on the couch with Brenda. Finally the other killer and one of the girls came out of a back room. Letty got up. "Okay," she announced, "party's over. Get out."

She went around the room rousing the men. Barney didn't move and she gave him an ungentle thump in the ribs with her toe. "Get up!" she commanded.

Billy roused himself and helped the very drunk Tomlain to his feet. Gradually they all dispersed, the girls yawning and heading for their rooms, the men out the door. Brenda was prompted to run after Billy and give him one last kiss on the porch.

Finally only Letty was left. She went around turning down kerosene lamps. Juno came in. "Please, Miss Letty, where I sleep?"

"Sleep in my room, Juno, go on now."

Then she herself turned to the rough stairs and climbed up to the little left story. Saulter's eyes were open when she turned the lock in the door and slipped into the room. It was a bright night and the moonlight streaming in through the small window made the room half lit. Letty slipped into a chair and sighed.

Saulter didn't speak, just turned his head to where he could see her. His face was emotionless.

She waited a second or two before she burst out. "Listen, don't look at me like that. Who the hell you think you are?"

"I'm not looking at you any way," he said. "I have no right to look at you or to think anything."

"You're damn right," she said, but she was slightly mollified.

"I just don't understand," he said.

"What don't you understand?"

"This place. You. The whole setup. This is . . ." he hesitated.

"A whorehouse? Sure it's a whorehouse. What'd you think it was, a library? And I'm a whore. So?"

"But here," he said. "Here in this place, here where there's nothing. I don't understand how it can be here."

She answered dryly. "Let's just say it's a private whorehouse. Set up to keep a few overgrown boys happy while they sit around waiting."

"Them?" he jerked his head in the direction of the saloon.

"Of course."

"And what are they doing here? In the middle of nowhere?"

"I told you, they're waiting."

"For what?"

"I don't know," she said, looking away.

"Letty . . ."

"Look, I said I don't know. And if I did I wouldn't tell you. And if I would I couldn't. You've got one thing to worry about—getting on your feet. You just lay there and rest for a couple of days and then ride the hell out of here and don't look back. I think I'd even go with you if I could get my money out of McGraw."

"Who is this McGraw? That's all I've heard."

"He's bad, that's who he is. Listen, stop asking so many questions and go to sleep."

But he wouldn't. Instead he pursued the questions. "What's around here to hold that kind of men? They're after only one thing—money. There's no towns around here. No gold mines. No cattle ranches. No gold shipments coming through from California. The closest thing is the railroads and they're still working on that. It couldn't be the railroad payroll. That'd take an army."

She suddenly got out of the chair, leaned down, and kissed him. "Shut up, Saulter. Go to sleep. I'm dead on my feet." She started to slump back in the chair, but he pulled the covers back on one side of the bed and looked at her.

She asked, "Even with what you think I've been doing downstairs?"

"Yes," he said.

"All right," she agreed. "But we're just going to sleep. You're too weak for anything else." She got up and took off her dress. She had on several petticoats. She got down to her Merry Widow underwear and then slid into bed beside Saulter.

He smiled slightly. "I may be a little rank. Haven't had much chance to take a bath lately."

"That's all right," she said, "you just smell like a man. And they don't all smell like that. Some can wash everyday and still stink. We'll give you a bath tomorrow. A whore's bath."

He looked over at her, her face very close to his. "What's a whore's bath?"

"That's the kind of bath you have to take in a house with a bunch of women and no tubs. A bucket of hot water and a lot of rubbing."

He smiled. "I might like that."

"You're getting better fast," she said dryly.

They were quiet for a moment, their eyes closed. Finally hers flickered open and she looked at his face in profile. "By the way, nobody touched me downstairs."

"I heard you cussing Tomlain."

"He tried. But that's all."

"Well . . ." he finally said, "that's another mistake he's made."

FIVE

WITH THE MID-MORNING sun came four men, riding across the snow field that led into the town. One rode in the lead; that as well as other things made him predominantly different from the rest. There were his clothes, a long coat and a flat crowned beaver hat, that were of better quality than those of the men with him. There was his horse and the trappings of his saddle and rigging. But the primary difference was in his carriage and his demeanor. There was a hawklike ruthlessness about his face, an intelligence in his eyes, and a cruel cut to his mouth that was made even more distinctive by the desolation of his surroundings.

As they came closer to the town the man in the lead began to slowly shift his eyes in a searching sweep of what lay ahead.

Barney saw them coming first. He'd gone out on the saloon porch to spit and breathe a little fresh air. As he stood there smoking, he glanced casually to his left, then straightened and studied hard. With them still a couple of hundred yards away he suddenly whirled and dashed into the saloon. The others were sitting around their table, drinking whiskey and finishing a fried steak. Barney came charging up. "It's McGraw," he cried. "McGraw and the rest are coming. Just up the road."

Billy smiled slightly. "Sit down, Barney. Take it easy else you'll have a convulsion."

Barney said, as he took a seat, "I just thought we ought to go out and meet him or something."

Billy laughed. "He'll find his way in."

Tomlain was chewing a mouthful of steak. "How far off is he?"

"Just a little piece," Barney said. He rubbed his hands together. "Boy, oh boy, looks like we gonna finally get this show on the road."

"About time," Tomlain said. He clattered his fork onto his plate. "I'm tired of sitting around this goddam town." He looked at Billy. "How long we been stuck here?"

Billy ran a hand through his hair. "Better than a month, anyway."

"Seems like a goddam year," Tomlain growled. He got up and walked behind the chair. "I tell you, I've about had it. We don't get this goddam action moving this time and I'm slam ass gonna bust."

Billy smiled. "You knew the rules when you got in, Ray. So did I."

"Yeah, but words is one thing. Hangin' around this goddam hole is something else." He licked his lips. "I wish I'd kept that goddam pilgrim around here to play with. Kill him a little every day."

"Well," Barney offered, "things will start to move now that Mister McGraw is back."

The riders came on, nearing the front of the store. The three trailing men were tough and ruthless and capable looking. They pulled up in front of the saloon and McGraw got down, dropping his reins like a man used to having someone else see to his horse. He climbed up the steps, not bothering to knock the snow off his clothing. As he opened the door and stepped into the room, the men at the table stood up, some promptly, some grudgingly, like Tomlain.

He stopped just inside the door. Slowly he took off his long saddle coat. Without looking he threw it over a nearby chair. "Well, gentlemen," he said, "I see you're keeping well." He got out a cigar and lit it, then started forward. "Let's all have a drink. Schmidt!"

"Yes, sir, Mister McGraw."

"Bottle of my private stock."

"Yes, sir!"

The other three men came trooping in the door. There was a round of handshakes and then the bottle appeared. "Now then," McGraw said. "I've had a long, hard ride. Let's not talk about business for the moment." He raised his glass. "But we will begin with a toast to sure success!"

Across the street, Saulter and Letty were still in bed. The room was dim and they still slept. A slight rap came at the door. They both opened their eyes. In another second the rap was more insistent. "What is it?" Letty called.

A voice on the other side of the door said, "Open up, Letty. Something you got to know."

"Hell," Letty exclaimed. She got up, being careful not to throw the covers off Saulter, and put on a robe. She unlocked the door and swung it back. It was Sheila.

"Letty," Sheila said, "it's McGraw. He's back. He's here."

"Where? In the house?"

"No," Sheila said, "they just rode in. They're in the saloon."

"All right," Letty said. She looked suddenly very tired. "All right, you go on now. Thanks."

She went to a chair and sat down, looking at Saulter. He pulled himself up on the bed. From the way he moved you could tell he was much better.

"I didn't think he'd come so soon," she said finally. "I thought we had at least two more days."

"It's bad, him coming?"

"Very bad," she said. She hesitated. "You're stronger?"

"Yes."

She looked at him for a long moment. "I think you ought to go."

"All right," he answered. He moved to throw the covers back and swing around.

"Not yet," she said. "For god's sake. Wait until dark."

"Why?"

"Why? So you can get away." She looked at him. "Look, you got it all wrong. I don't want you to leave for my sake, but for yours. I want you to get away from here. It's going to be all different now that McGraw's back."

"I can't leave," he said. "I can get out of your house, but I'm not going anywhere."

"Why not?"

"I've still got some business to tend to here."

Letty's mouth tightened. "What kind of business? You don't have any business here. Your business is to get away from this place."

"Not until I tend to this."

"What?"

"Tomlain."

"Oh god," she said, throwing up her hands. "I might have known! Tomlain." She looked at him in disgust. "Listen, there'd be nine of them now that McGraw is back. You can't get at Tomlain. Forget it."

"No."

"You're crazy."

"Nevertheless."

They stared at each other for a moment. She broke the silence. "What would you do?"

"I'd hide in the barn or somewhere until I could catch him."

"You really mean this?"

"Yes."

"All right," she said, "but you're just going to get yourself killed."

"Perhaps. But I doubt it."

She stood up and began dressing. He watched her. He said, "I'll slip out the back."

"No you won't," she said. "You'll stay here at least through tomorrow. At least you can rest."

He lay back in bed, consenting.

She finished dressing and faced him. "But look . . ." She hesitated. "Things are going to be a little different now."

"All right."

"McGraw will be sleeping over here. In this house."

"All right."

"He'll be sleeping in my room."

He looked at her.

"I'll have to be sleeping with him."

He nodded slowly. "All right. I don't own you."

"He does," she said harshly. "Bought and paid for."

"That's your business."

"Goddam you," she said. She went to the door and opened it. But she stopped and turned back. "If you've got to kill someone why don't you kill McGraw?"

He answered her seriously. "I've got no quarrel with the man."

She smiled, "That's what you think. I'll send Juno up with some food." She shook her head. "This is crazy as hell. We're all going to get ourselves killed."

He waited until she was gone and then slowly got out of bed and stood up. He was wearing just the bottoms to his long underwear. Slowly, he stretched and bent, feeling for the pain. He was a little unsteady at first, but you could see him gritting it through and willing his body to obey. He raised his hands and looked at them, clenching and unclenching his fists and wiggling his fingers. Finally he got his pants and a shirt out of the chiffonier and put them on. It cost him an effort, but you could see he was much improved. Finally he pulled on his boots.

After that he didn't do anything for a few seconds except sit on the edge of the bed. Then he arose and got his big gun. He unsheathed it and stood looking at it for a moment. It was a magnificent weapon, almost six feet long. It broke down at the breech like a shotgun and breech loaded, shooting one shell at a time. He laid it on the bed, then reached in the closet and brought out a heavy leather pouch. He sat down on the bed and took a huge shell out of the pouch. He slipped that in the breech of the rifle, snapped it shut, and lay the gun aside. Now from the pouch, he took out the various paraphernalia for reloading cartridges: the brass, the huge bullet heads, the powder. He settled down to the meticulous task of furnishing himself a large supply of ammunition. As he made each shell he laid it carefully on the bed.

Over in the saloon the level was getting low in the bottle of whiskey. McGraw downed what was in his glass with a satisfied sigh. He looked over at the bar. "Mr. Schmidt, leave us please. And take that boy with you. We can look after ourselves for the time being."

"Yes, sir." Schmidt took off his apron, put on a coat, and motioned violently for Chiffo to follow him. McGraw watched until they'd gone. Then he directed Barney to step to the door and make sure they were not listening just outside. "They gone, Mister McGraw," Barney said. He came back to the table.

McGraw looked around at the faces of his men. "Well, gentlemen, it looks as if we're about to go to work."

Billy asked. "Close, huh?"

McGraw took a map out of his pocket, unrolled it, and spread it on the table. "The two lines are only about thirty miles apart right now and moving at the rate of four miles a day each. They should make the join up in about a week. . . ." He pointed at the map. "About right here."

Billy looked. "Promontory Point" he said. "Promontory Point, Utah. Has a nice sound to it. That a town?"

"No, just a geographical name the railroads have picked out for where they intend to meet. Now, I don't know when the ceremonial hookup is going to be made—"

Barney broke in. "They really going to drive a gold spike? I mean a real gold spike?"

"Yes," McGraw said, annoyed. "But that's not our concern. As I say, I don't know when the ceremonial hookup will be—that'll depend on Washington and the governmental officials—but I want to move out of here in a couple of days and establish a camp within striking distance of Promontory Point."

Billy hesitated, then interrupted. "Wanted to, uh, ask you about the getaway arrangements, Mister McGraw. Has any more been done on that?" He laughed. "That's of some interest to us."

McGraw nodded. "Good point." He stuck a cigar in his mouth. "I'm going to have horse relay stations set up every ten miles going south. There'll be four, with top-quality horses ready for every man. By the time you've used those up you ought to have outrun any immediate pursuit. Even if there is any." He looked around at them through a wreath of smoke. "You understand, of course, that if everything goes according to plan there won't be any pursuit. In that great crowd and turmoil it will be impossible to know where the shots came from. And the soldiers and other guards should be in total confusion. But I'm making every precaution that every possibility is taken care of."

"Well, it's just that it's so big," Billy said depreciatingly. "I mean, the target is a pretty big man and it might stir up a hornets' nest."

"I understand and I agree. The final arrangements on the getaway will be completed while we are in our forward camp. Every man will be completely looked after. I'm not expecting any of you to take foolhardy chances in this enterprise. As you know, every one of you will be out of the country with all the money you'll ever need. Plans right now are for you to take a steamship out of Tampico, but that will all be finalized at the appropriate time. But I assure you that nothing will be left to chance."

"We appreciate that," Billy said.

"Now," McGraw said, "let's get down to the actual plan of battle. I believe we can consider it set and it's almost exactly as forecast." He took up another roll of plans and spread it out on the table, anchoring the corners with bottles and glasses. "This is just a rough sketch, but it will do to give you all the details. Here"—his finger traced a set of pencil tracks—"is the line of the tracks. Both east and west. Here"—he pointed to an X—"is where they will meet. That is absolute and certain, it's been selected by both railroads in advance so the various paraphernalia for the celebration can be erected. They will arrange to meet there and join the two tracks." He made a sweeping motion with his finger. "All the country around is rocky and broken and very rough. Here"—he stabbed out a finger to some marks— "is where we have been so very fortunate. This is a butte that commands a view of the joining point and will provide a clear field of fire at our target. It is from here that Mister Tomlain will make the shot that will make us all very rich." He looked around at them and smiled slowly. "Believe me, gentlemen, it's perfect."

They mirrored his smile, looking over and grinning at Tomlain, who was beginning to swell with the attention. McGraw went on. "The distance is three hundred fifty-two yards. We have measured it and remeasured it. From that distance and with the necessary elevation to give him an absolutely clear shot, I don't see how Ray Tomlain can miss. Do you, gentlemen?"

They said, "Ain't no chance!" And "By god, that money's good as ours!" And "Look out, you South American señoritas!" And "Best rifle shot in the world!"

McGraw grinned at Tomlain. "Well, Ray? Look all right to you?"

Tomlain cocked his head back. "You give me a clear shot with that big .405 of mine and I can hit any man at four hundred yards. Any place you want him hit."

Billy clapped him on the back. "That a boy, Ray."

McGraw nodded, pleased. "I think we're in good hands, gentlemen." He smoothed his map. "But, of course, any plan, to be really good, must have a backup. And we'll have two. Of course

Billy and William will be up on the butte with Ray. Billy, as you all know, is the backup shot for Tomlain. If anything happens to Ray, Billy will take the rifle and make the shot. William is there for protection and covering fire in case it should become necessary. But we don't expect that. From what I can gather the security is going to be very poor, almost nonexistent. There will be a general air of drunkenness and gaiety with people running in every which direction. Like all government functions, total confusion should reign. All to our advantage. Now," he said, looking around, "if for some reason, Ray should miss, or not kill his target . . ."

Tomlain broke in, a swagger in his voice. "Well, you can make these here other plans if you want to," he said, "but you're just wastin' your time and breath. Old Ray ain't gonna miss. And that big bore rifle of mine is gonna kill him if I nick his eyebrow."

"Well said, Ray," McGraw commented, "but we've got to give these other men a feeling they're earning their money. Now Barney, of course, is in charge of the horses. He'll be holding the main group for Jackhammer and Runt. They will pose as trainmen. You'll approach the spike-driving ceremonies under that guise, working your way very close. If the shot is, for some reason, not lethal, then you, Jackhammer, are to begin firing into the target with your pistol. Runt will be your protection. Clemson and Ellis are to be dressed as Federal troopers. You will work your way close from the other side. Your mission is the same as Jackhammer's and Runt's though you'll be using the government-issue carbines you'll be provided. Now—" He looked around at their faces.

Runt made a sound with his mouth. "Hmmm. Sure hope we don't have to do that. In all that crowd? How we get away?"

McGraw said, "That's what it seems like here. But you must realize that at the scene there will be total confusion. Any number of men will have their guns out and will be firing. At anything. We'll be the only ones with a plan and with preparation. The rest will be total confusion. I can assure you, you'll be able to make your escape easily in the mass pandemonium that's going to result as soon as Ray's rifle sounds the first shot. From then on, of course, we'll be on swift horses and what little pursuit, if any, will quickly be left far behind."

"Sounds good to me," Billy said.

McGraw said, "Of course these are the plans in general. We'll work out all the final details in advance camp. All right?"

They chorused assent, looking around at each other and grinning.

McGraw drew an expansive breath. "And how has it been with you men? Been treated all right?"

"No complaints," Billy said.

But Tomlain put in, "Ain't been exactly where I wanted to go to root." He tried to make a joke out of it, but it came out rough.

McGraw nodded. "I understand. I appreciate your patience. But I'm sure that you can each understand the necessity for us all staying together in one place out of the reach of interested ears. I trust each of you implicitly, but you can never tell when a man might get too much of this"—he held up the bottle—"in him and go to talking when he shouldn't. This proposition has been too important to take any chances on. I think I've done my best to see to your comfort."

Billy grinned. "We understand, Mister McGraw."

"Now then, been any disturbances? Anything to report?"

Barney began, "Well, there was this one fellow come in. He . . ."

But at a fierce scowl from Tomlain he broke off.

"What?" Mr. McGraw asked. "What fellow?"

Billy put in, "Just a stranger passing through. Hunter or miner. He didn't stay. And didn't anybody talk to him."

McGraw looked at them sharply. "You're sure? You didn't arouse any curiosity?"

"Not a chance," Billy said. He smiled and looked at Tomlain. "I seen to it special. Guy went on his way without a care in the world."

"Good," McGraw said, nodding. "That's the way we want to keep it." He leaned back in his chair and stretched. "Well, let's drink another bottle of whiskey and then I think I'll go across and get some rest."

Barney guffawed. "Them women ain't going to let you rest, Mr. McGraw."

McGraw smiled. "And how are the ladies? Been seeing they're satisfied?"

"Oh, yes," Barney assured him.

"And how's Letty?"

"She's fine," Billy answered quickly, looking at Tomlain. "Just find and looking for you back."

"Good. Barney, get another bottle of whiskey."

• • •

It was late afternoon. Saulter was still sitting on the side of his bed, patiently making cartridges. He had a huge pile stacked up, maybe a hundred. Letty came in without knocking. She had a piece of beefsteak on a plate. She laid it on the bed and stood watching him. A certain reserve had now come between them because of where she would be sleeping that night.

"You going to use that big rifle on Tomlain?"

"No," he answered, without looking up at her.

"Then why are you making all the bullets?"

He shrugged, still not looking at her. "It's something to pass the time."

She went over to the window and stood, staring out, looking at the front of Schmidt's saloon. "McGraw hasn't come over yet," she said idly.

He didn't say anything.

She continued staring out the window. "Be dark in two hours."

He went on making cartridges.

She turned. "I'm having Juno fix you up a sack of provisions."

He looked up at her finally, "What for?"

"Because," she said, "you're getting out of here as soon as it gets dark. You're going to get on your horse and get the hell away from here. You're really not strong enough for it yet, but it will be a lot healthier for you than staying around here."

"I can't do that, Letty," he told her steadily.

"Dammit!" she swore. "You don't know what you're up against! Forget Tomlain! Get away from this place."

He looked at her calmly. "What am I up against, Letty?"

"I can't tell you that," she said violently. "But it's more than one man can handle. I don't care how good a man he is, he wouldn't have a chance against that over there." She pointed toward the window.

"Who are they?" he asked softly. "What's going on?"

"I can't tell you, dammit! But I can tell you they won't let you kill Tomlain. They can't afford to. He's too important to them."

"I don't have any choice, Letty."

"Yes, you do. Go, go, leave! While you can. If they catch you back here they'll kill you that quick!" She snapped her fingers.

"You don't answer any of my questions, Letty. Why not?"

"I'll answer this one. You don't have a chance. Those are killers over there. Eight of them. Hired special. The best. Gathered from all over by Mister McGraw. Every one a specialist at his job. Including McGraw."

"Who's McGraw? What's his business?"

"His business is doing favors. Handling things for people. For money, lots of money. Dammit, look around you. Can't you see how big this thing is? They've set up a cathouse and a saloon just to keep hired killers content while they wait. Whiskey and women. Now, dammit, go tonight."

"I'll be gone tomorrow, Letty."

She sat down on the bed beside him and took his face in her hands. "Look, Saulter, I don't know you, don't even know anything about you. But I

don't want you dead, do you hear? Please, listen to
me." She leaned forward and kissed him softly.
"Look, in a couple of weeks I'll be back in
Phoenix. Go down there and wait for me." She
kissed him again.

"I'll be gone tomorrow," he said steadily.

She sighed and got up. "You let that sun rise on
you here in the morning and you'll be buried
before it goes down."

"Maybe," he said. "But I don't think so."

She went to the door. "I'm going to send Juno
up with the food anyway. She's got to sleep in
here tonight." She looked at him a long moment.
"Goodbye, Saulter. Change your mind and go."

He watched her until the door closed. Finally
he took up the plate of beef and began to eat.
There was a bottle of whiskey on the floor by his
bed and he uncorked that and took a long pull. He
looked at the far wall, his eyes and his thoughts
turned inward. He sat there thinking for a long
time. Logically he knew that he should ride on,
leave the mess that Sunshine represented. But
there was Tomlain to be settled with and then
there were those other men and what they were
doing. It was none of his affair, but he kept
thinking it would be wrong, somehow, to just ride
away from it. He didn't like the feel of the place,
didn't like it at all. What a strange situation, he
thought to himself. Finally he sighed and took
another drink of whiskey. Well, there was still
Tomlain. He didn't know quite how he'd arrange
that, but it had to be settled. He expected he'd just
have to depend on luck and opportunity. That was
all part of hunting and he was used to that.

Very late that night he was still sitting just so, in the chair, fully dressed. Juno was in the bed, asleep. It had frightened her to come in and sleep with the big American in the room, but Letty had made her and he'd smiled at her. Now he just sat, waiting. He had his pistol in his lap and his other gear was all packed and stacked beside him. He still had no plans. What he probably thought he'd do would be to saddle up and then wait for Tomlain to come out. Then he'd kill him. He couldn't fight all of them and he wouldn't be fool enough to try so he'd have to find a way to isolate Tomlain. But he didn't know quite how he was going to do that.

There was suddenly a tiny thump against the wall, just outside, by the tiny window. Saulter was immediately alert. He brought his pistol to the ready, then eased up and flattened himself against the wall. There came a light rapping on the glass. It was repeated. Juno stirred, but didn't waken. Slowly the window was raised from the outside. As it opened a breath of cold air came into the room. Saulter raised his pistol, ready to bring it down on the head of whoever was about to come in. Cautiously the intruder stuck his head into the room. Then he began to wiggle in over the ledge. As he got his upper body into the room Saulter saw that it was Chiffo. He holstered his gun and suddenly reached out and grabbed the boy by the shoulders, jerked him the rest of the way in the room, and slammed him to the floor, putting his hand over the boy's mouth.

The boy's frightened eyes stared at him. Saulter put his face close to Chiffo's. In a fierce whisper he asked him, "What are you doing in here, boy? Is that your girlfriend?" He jerked his head toward the still sleeping Juno.

Chiffo nodded yes. He was very frightened.

"Did you know I was here?"

The boy shook his head.

"If I take my hand off your mouth are you going to keep quiet?"

The boy nodded a frantic yes.

"All right," Saulter said. He slowly removed his hand. As he did Chiffo said, in a normal voice, "Goddam, meester, you scare . . ."

But he got no further before Saulter clamped his hand back on the boy's mouth. "I said be quiet," he whispered fiercely. "Keep your voice down."

When he took his hand away this time Chiffo whispered also. "Damn, meester, I thought they kill you. What you doin' in this cathouse?"

"Just be quiet," Saulter told him. "And don't move. Stay just where you are." He got up slowly and sat back in the chair, looking at the boy. After a moment he said, "Well, you've done it now. What am I going to do with you?"

"You got a little wheesky for me?" Chiffo said.

Without speaking Saulter reached down, got the bottle, uncorked it, and gave it to the boy. He took such a long drink that Saulter had to take the bottle back. "Now sit there and be quiet," Saulter told him, "while I figure out what to do with you. This may be bad luck or good. I just ain't figured it out yet."

Saulter and Chiffo sat up all night, sometimes sipping at the whiskey, but mostly just waiting.

In his mind Saulter had turned over, then rejected, several plans of action. But as it began to come light, he spoke to Chiffo for the first time in several hours.

"I got a little job for you, Chiffo."

"What kind of job, señor? Does it pay wheesky?"

"It'll pay plenty of whiskey. Do you like Tomlain?"

"Tomlain!" The boy's face showed sudden fear. "I don't want no job with Meester Tomlain."

"All you got to do is take a message to him. You can do that, can't you?"

"I don't know," the boy said slowly. "*No sé*—what kind of message?"

"I'll tell you that later," Saulter said. He got up. "Com'on, we're going outside. But take it slow and don't make a sound." He began picking up his gear and the big rifle. He gave one knapsack to Chiffo to carry and lastly took up the whiskey bottle. "Let's go," he said. He opened the door and they slipped out in the darkened hall. Slowly and carefully they went down the stairs, moving one step at a time. A board creaked under Chiffo's foot and Saulter looked back at him. Then they came to the living room and Saulter stopped, undecided. It was dim and dark in the room. Slowly he moved over to the front door and eased it open. With the door just cracked he looked cautiously outside. Nothing was stirring. Gently he eased the door back, stopping when it creaked. Quietly, he and Chiffo passed through and Saulter closed the door. They went down the steps, Saulter leading the way, and turned around the building toward the little barn in back. Their boots crunched quietly in the crusted snow. It was very quiet and very dim; dawn was a half hour away. Chiffo was nervous and frightened, but there was nothing for him to do but follow Saulter.

They went in the barn. Saulter had to halt a moment to let his eyes accustom themselves to the dark. Finally he was able to pick out a few dim stalls. He looked in a couple until he found his horse. The animal looked around, recognizing him and started to whinny. Saulter walked up beside the animal, rubbing his neck and talking softly. "Find my saddle," he told Chiffo.

"How come your horse is here?" Chiffo asked him.

"Just get the saddle."

Quietly, in the dark, they saddled and bridled the horse. Saulter packed him with his several knapsacks and lastly rammed the big rifle into its boot.

"You leave now?" Chiffo asked him.

"No," Saulter said. "Not yet. Come on over here."

With the whiskey bottle in his hand he led the boy over to the main door. He cracked it just enough to see out and then sat down, motioning for Chiffo to sit across from him.

He looked at the boy. "When it gets light I'm going to want you to go wake Tomlain up and give him a message."

The boy shook his head, frightened again. "No, señor. I much afraid of Tomlain. He keel me I wake him up."

"No, he won't," Saulter told him. "You're going

to give him a message from Mister McGraw. He won't get mad about that."

The boy swallowed visibly. "I even more scairt of Meester McGraw."

"Well, he ain't ever gonna know," Saulter said. "Because if you do like I tell you, you won't never have to be afraid of Tomlain anymore."

"*Cómo?*"

"Because I'm going to kill Mister Tomlain."

"Keel? Meester Tomlain?"

"Yes. Can you take a message for me?"

The boy was uncertain. "*Yo no sé.* I don't know."

"Here," Saulter said. He handed the boy the bottle. "Have a little whiskey." The boy drank, his eyes watching Saulter over the end of the upturned bottle.

"That's enough," Saulter said. He reached out and took the bottle. "This job is going to pay plenty of whiskey," he told the boy.

"Plenty whiskey?"

Saulter held up two fingers. "Two bottles."

"Two bottles wheesky?"

"And all you have to do is go wake up Mister Tomlain and tell him Mister McGraw wants to see him. It'll be easy."

"I scairt," Chiffo declared.

"Have some more," Saulter offered. "You do right and no one will ever know. Tomlain will be dead and he won't be able to say."

"What if he keel you?"

Saulter said, simply, "That's not going to happen."

"He plenty bad man. Maybe he keel you. Then what am I do?"

"That ain't going to happen," Saulter said firmly. "Have another drink. It's starting to come light."

They waited until it came full day. Then Saulter rose and opened the door a little wider. "Com'on, boy," he said. Chiffo got up reluctantly.

"I scairt," the boy said.

"Nothing to be scared of," Saulter assured him. "You do exactly like I tell you and everything will be all right."

"Where my plenty wheesky?"

"Here," Saulter said. He dug down in his pocket and came out with three silver dollars. "Here's your pay. That's the same as two bottles." He took the boy by the shoulders and steered him through the barn entrance. "Now you go over there and wake Tomlain up. Just tell him Mister McGraw sent you for him, that Mister McGraw wants to see him in the ladies' house. Do it as quiet as you can and try not to wake anyone else up. Tell him McGraw said to bring his gun and hurry. You got that?"

"I still afeered."

"Have another pull then." Saulter gave him the bottle and let him take a long drink. "Hurry now, everybody will be getting up pretty soon. Run."

He stood watching until Chiffo was halfway across to the bunkhouse. Then he quickly went back, made sure his horse was ready, and then went out the barn through a side door. He walked behind the women's house and to a position where he could peek around the corner and see the bunkhouse. As he waited he checked his pistol, putting a sixth shell in it where he'd normally only carry five. He worked the action several times, making sure it was free and easy.

Chiffo had gone into the bunkhouse. Saulter waited, pistol in hand. A few long moments passed and then Chiffo came out. He stopped, looked hesitantly toward the barn and then scuttled in the back door of the saloon. After another moment Tomlain came out. He was tucking in his shirt, carrying his gun belt in his hand. Saulter watched him from around the corner of the building. Tomlain stopped once to buckle his gun belt and then came on for the women's house.

He was perhaps twenty yards away when Saulter suddenly stepped out into the open. He had the pistol in his hand, hanging down by his side. He said sharply, "Tomlain!" The word cracked like a shot in the cold quietness of the morning. Tomlain jumped and then swung quickly around. He stared, astonishment and surprise written all over his face. "What the . . ." he began and then switched to, "You! Goddam! You!"

Saulter held the pistol so that it was half hidden behind his leg. "You made a mistake, Tomlain," Saulter said. His voice was as cold and hard as the packed snow. "The worst you've ever made."

Tomlain still seemed to be held by surprise. But in a second, a slow, ugly smile began to spread over his face. "Well, well, well," he said. He licked his lips, dry and cracking in the cold wind.

"Boy, I never thought I'd get another chance at you. This is going to be like getting to kill you twice." He turned and started walking directly for the hunter.

Saulter watched him narrowly, gauging the distance. He didn't intend to give Tomlain much chance.

Tomlain was talking as he advanced. "Snake shooter, you can't seem to learn where you ain't wanted. Well, now you ain't got nobody like little Billy to stick up for you. I reckon I'll teach you the hardest lesson you ever learned."

At ten yards he suddenly stopped and his hand flashed as he started out with his pistol. But Saulter had anticipated the move and his arm swung up even as Tomlain was reaching for his weapon. He sighted down his long arm and fired an instant before Tomlain. The bullet took the gunman square in the chest and flipped him over backwards, his pistol firing harmlessly as he hit the snow. For a second he flinched and threshed and then he was still. Saulter walked slowly toward him, his pistol held loosely in his hand. At the body he stood looking down for a second. Already blood was staining the blinding whiteness of the snow. Deliberately Saulter flipped up the chamber of his revolver and ejected the spent shell. It bounced off Tomlain's chest and then rolled into the snow. Without another look Saulter turned, sticking his revolver in his belt, and made for the barn at a deliberate pace. He knew that the shots must have been heard and that men would be coming, but he would not run. There should be time, he thought, to get on his horse and ride away before the men in the bunk-house could get up and get organized and come out.

He passed the back of the women's house. For a fleeting second he thought of Letty, hating the thought of leaving her with these men. But that was just a reaction to her kindness. This was where she'd been when he'd found her. The barn and his horse were only a few steps further.

At that instant a man suddenly came flying out the back door of the women's house. Saulter caught a glimpse out of the corner of his eye and whirled, his hand reaching instinctively for his pistol. But the man had a Winchester rifle already leveled and aimed at Saulter's chest. "Hold it!" the man yelled. He was down on one knee, the rifle steady. For an instant Saulter considered, conflict was working in his face. "Hold it!" the man yelled again. "Goddammit, you move and I'll shoot you. Get your hands on your head!"

Slowly and deliberately he did as the man told him.

"Mister McGraw!" the man shouted without taking his eyes off Saulter. "Mister McGraw!" He looked at Saulter. "Who the hell are you, bronc? And what the hell you doing here? Boy, you done got yourself in a mess of trouble." He yelled for McGraw again.

Across the way the rest of the crew came boiling out of the bunkhouse. Some of them were dressed, but most were still in underwear, hopping across the snow while they pulled on boots and strapped on gun belts. They came charging across the snow, Billy in the lead. When they got to Tomlain's body they instinctively paused for a moment. Billy knelt to make sure he was really dead. Then they came on, at a run.

At that instant McGraw came out the back door of the women's house. From his clothing it was obvious he'd dressed hurriedly. He was wearing a suit of good quality, but no vest or tie. He had an enormous buffalo coat thrown over his shoulders like a cape. Behind him the women of the house slowly gathered at the door. As he walked toward Saulter, an outraged expression distorted his face.

Barney was the first to reach Saulter from the bunkhouse group. He stopped and stared open-mouthed. "My god," he exclaimed, "it's the old boy that was supposed to have froze to death!"

McGraw put a cigar in his mouth, staring hard at Saulter. Billy had come running up by now. McGraw said sharply, "Who is this man?"

Before Bill could speak, Barney blurted out, "He's the pilgrim that had a run-in with Tomlain. Now he's killed Tomlain."

McGraw looked at him. "He's done what?"

"He's killed Ray Tomlain, Mister McGraw." Barney gestured behind him. "He's layin' out there with a hole in him as big as a boot and this one must have done it."

McGraw drew slowly on his cigar and stared at Saulter. "*He* killed Tomlain, *Ray Tomlain?*"

They were all there by then and they stood ranged around McGraw and Saulter and the man with the rifle. "I guess he done it, Mister McGraw," Billy said. "Tomlain's layin' out there with a hole in his chest and this here man has got a pistol." He reached over with those words and jerked the revolver out of Saulter's belt. "It even looks straight. Ray's gun is out."

As if to see for himself, McGraw walked through the group and looked across the snow at Tomlain. Then he turned back and stared again at Saulter. "Goddammit!" he swore. "Goddammit to hell!" He turned and looked at the group around him. "Do you fools have any idea what this means? How in the hell did you allow this to happen?"

Barney said, "Mister McGraw, we didn't have no idea this feller had come back. We thought he was long gone."

Letty had come out on the back porch. She slowly sifted her way through the other women and came to the front. Her eyes went to Saulter. He was standing there like a stone, his hands still over his head. He glanced briefly at her and then quickly looked away.

McGraw took the cigar out of his mouth and threw it in the snow. His face was contorted with anger. "Who is this man?" He turned and pointed a finger at Saulter. "How did he get here? What's he doing here?"

Barney spoke first. "It was like I was trying to tell you yesterday, Mister McGraw. This is the one through here a few days back. But we thought he was dead. We thought Tomlain beat him to death with his fists. I don't indeed know what he's doing standing here today."

The rifleman, who had relaxed his vigilance, lifted his rifle again. "You want me to tend to him right now, Mister McGraw? I can take him out behind the barn if you don't want the ladies to see."

McGraw didn't bother to answer, just went on staring hard at Saulter. "First, I want some answers. I want to know how this man came to be here and to shoot Tomlain." He looked at the other men. "How did you allow this to happen? Billy?"

Billy looked down at the ground.

"Barney? You seem to want to talk."

"He come through here hurt or something. Wanted to stay, but Tomlain made him leave. Whipped up on him, don't you know? We all thought he'd took on off. Supposed to have been killed. Froze or somethin' cause his horse came back. Supposed to have been gone three or four days. But here he is. Beats hell out of me." Barney looked closely at Saulter. "Thing is, where's he been? Look at him. He don't look like he's been layin' out in no snowbank. Looks considerably better'n when he left."

One of the other gunmen spoke up. "Say, I hadn't thought on that. I believe Barney's right. He don't look like he's had a flake of snow on him. He ain't been holed up out in the hills and we searched every building in this town. Where in hell's the sonofabitch been?"

McGraw listened, drawing intently on a fresh cigar. "Am I to understand that this man might well have been around here for the last several days? *Listening!* Listening to our plans!" A little blood vessel began to throb in his temple as the anger worked its slow way through him. McGraw prided himself on never losing his head, but he could feel his control slipping as he contemplated the ruin these fool gunmen might have created. He breathed out a hard breath. "Somebody better goddam well get me some answers right now. Have you fools been letting him sleep in the bunkhouse? Have you been drinking with him? Do you idiots have any conception of how much money is at stake here?" He looked at them, glaring, and again they all hung their heads. He whirled on Saulter. "Well, sir," he said with exaggerated calm, "you've apparently been my unwelcome guest. I own this town. I own these people here. I don't owe you a goddam thing except a bullet if you don't tell me what I want to know, quickly. Who are you and what are you doing here?"

Saulter turned his head slowly and stared at him.

"Goddam you, answer me!"

Saulter didn't speak.

"Where have you been? In Schmidt's? In one of the barns?"

Saulter glanced away, toward the snow-covered hills. Then he leaned his head down and spit deliberately between his boots.

McGraw took a quick step forward and slapped him sharply in the face. "By god, don't you come that on me, you sonofabitch! I asked you a question. You just think you won't answer." He whirled to the rifleman. "William, cock that weapon."

The man slowly brought his gun up, the muzzle only feet from Saulter's chest. With a deliberate thumb he pulled the hammer back.

"Now, sir," McGraw said to Saulter.

Saulter stared back.

"Are you a fool? Do you want to join Mister Tomlain out there?" He pointed. "Believe me, it matters not to me whether I shoot you or not. What you have to tell me is not even particularly important except it might indicate which one of my men here has been negligent. That's all your silence is doing, protecting one of them. Answer me, damn you!"

Slowly Saulter's jaw worked. "Go to hell."

McGraw hesitated only a second. "All right. Have it your own way." He turned to the rifleman. "Shoot him."

In that instant Letty stepped forward. "Hold on," she said. McGraw turned to her. She took another step forward. "All right, McGraw. He's been here. I've been hiding him."

Everything stopped. McGraw's hand was still up to signal the rifleman. It hung there in the air while he stared at Letty for a long second. Barney let out his breath. "I be go to hell," he said.

McGraw turned to face Letty. "I beg your pardon?"

"He was hurt and sick," she said. "He was dying." She jerked her head toward where Tomlain lay in the snow. "Your damn bully left him beat to death out in the street. I took him in like you would a stray cat. That's all. He don't know nothing about nothing."

He nodded slowly. "Your philanthropy overwhelms me, madame. I didn't know it was part of your profession."

"Listen," she said, bridling her anger, "the hell

with that kind of talk. He was wounded and I took him in to nurse for a day or two. That's all. Just to let him get his strength back and put him on the road. I didn't know this other was going to happen." Again she jerked her head in the direction of Tomlain. "But what could you expect? Your goddam bully nearly killed him. Anything Tomlain got he had coming. Don't blame this man for it."

"Don't blame him?" He looked at her quizzically. "Madame, have you lost what little mind you ever had? Who shall I blame then?"

"Blame Tomlain. If he'd left the man alone this wouldn't have happened."

"Do you think we're schoolboys playing at some game, woman? What is this talk from you? You amaze me." He reached up and stroked a hand across his mouth. "But I will tend to you later. We're going to have to discuss your part in this." He turned around to where Saulter was still standing. "And now you, sir." He walked to the front of the hunter and faced him. "You've done me much harm. Perhaps irreparable harm. I don't know how much yet. I'm going to have to study the situation. I'm going to have you killed now, but I want you to understand I don't do it maliciously, if that's any comfort to you. There's no pay in that sort of thing. But you have done me harm and for that there's got to be a settlement." He turned to the rifleman. "William, walk this man out behind that barn and shoot him."

Letty said, "McGraw! Don't!"

He took his cigar out of his mouth and looked at her. "Well, well, well. This is deeper than I thought. Now you're pleading for his life. What do you offer, your virtue?"

Before she could answer Billy cleared his throat. "Mister McGraw . . ." He took off his hat as a sign of respect. "Mister McGraw, I wonder if you wouldn't let me talk to you about this feller. I know you ain't the kind to go rushing up no box canyons and I think I might tell you something could be of considerable interest."

"Oh?" McGraw asked questioningly.

"Yessir."

"Such as?"

Billy looked uncomfortable. "I'd rather not get into it out here in the open like this, sir. But I will say that he was with the railroads. . . ."

"Oh?" McGraw said.

"Yessir. He was a meat hunter for them. He's got a sharpshooter's rifle."

"Ah?"

"And we are a man short now that he's killed Tomlain." He hesitated. "I'd think he killed Ray Tomlain in a fair fight from the looks of it and the man that can do that . . ." He trailed off.

"What do you suggest?" McGraw asked.

Billy shrugged. "Well, why don't we go on over to the saloon and have some breakfast and let me tell you my idea. Hell, you can shoot him just as easy an hour from now as here on the spot."

McGraw drew on his cigar, considering. "A good point."

Billy, his confidence growing, said, "I think you ought to listen to what I can tell you before you decide."

McGraw stood a moment thinking, drawing on

his cigar. Finally he turned to the rifleman. "William, search the gentleman for any other weapons he might have. Be thorough."

While Saulter, standing calm but tense, was being roughly patted down, McGraw turned again to Letty. "You bewilder me, madame. I am hard-pressed to understand your actions. I think you may have some serious accounting to render later. Wait inside." The words were calm and polite, but the threat was no less real.

"Oh, go to hell," she said, her anger still up.

"Probably," he agreed, "as will you." He looked at Saulter, then back at Letty. "Perhaps in a much sooner time, madame, than you'd planned. Unless my man over here has better suggestions." He turned to face Saulter. "You go inside with the women. You seem to like it in there, so you just go inside and rest while we decide your case." He looked sharply around. "Barney! William! Put this man inside the house and patrol both doors. If he gets away I'll hold you accountable."

"Yes, sir!" Barney said, coming forward. "Do we go inside, Mister McGraw?"

With a bemused expression on his face McGraw turned to look at Letty. "No. There are only two doors. Stay outside and watch them. And the windows. Inside you might be seduced into letting stray cats run. You'll be safer outside." He said the major part of the sentence looking at Letty. Then he turned to Billy. "Let's go have some breakfast."

As they walked off, Barney and William came forward and prodded Saulter toward the back door of the women's house. "Just move it, boy," William said. "Just get on in there." Saulter went reluctantly, slowly. As he passed Letty he turned his face to hers. She stared back. There was nothing in either expression.

He went into the house at the point of William's rifle, and the door was shut behind him. "I'll take the back and you get the front," William said.

The women opened the door and went in slowly, looking back over their shoulders as William settled down in the snow with his rifle across his knees. Inside, Saulter walked into the parlor and went to the front window. He stood there, staring out. Letty and the other women came into the room. She turned facing them, and said sharply, "Go to your rooms! Now! I'll call you later."

Saulter was still standing at the parlor window, staring at the saloon across the street. The room was dim, but dappled with the early morning sunshine. Letty came up behind him. They stood there silently for a moment. Finally she spoke. "Well, you've done it now."

He would not look at her.

"I warned you."

"All right."

"No. It's not all right. You could have left. You could have run. You could have left Tomlain alone."

He said, "Listen, I did what I had to do. You let a man do what he did to me and let it go and you're walking away the rest of your life. I don't run."

"You goddam fool," she said bitterly. "They'll

be coming across here in half an hour to shoot you. Is that what you had to do?"

"It's none of your concern."

"What?" Her voice bit out like the cold.

He turned to look at her. "It's none of your concern," he said again.

She put her fists to her hips for a second. They were knotted. For a moment she seemed to almost shake with rage. He waited calmly for what he could see coming. "None of my *concern!*" With two swift, strong strokes she slapped him on both sides of his face. "None of my concern!"

He stared at her unflinching.

"Oh, go to hell," she burst out. And then she turned away. She walked a few feet back into the parlor and started to cry. Finally, he spoke.

"Letty . . ."

"Oh, shut up," she said.

He went near her, putting out a hand to touch her shoulder. She shrugged it off. "Look, I'm sorry," he said awkwardly. "You've been damn fine to me . . ." He let the sentence trail off. "I don't know what to say."

She turned on him. "If you've got anything you want to say, any last words, you better make them damn fast. You don't know what you're in with. This bunch will kill you like flicking out a candle. I told you you were into something bigger than you knew, but you wouldn't listen to me. Now, goddammit, you're going to pay for it."

"What, Letty? What?" He took her by the shoulders and whirled her to face him. "Dammit, tell me what you mean. No more of these half hints. I got to know what's going on."

She faced him for a long moment. Finally she shrugged in resignation, breaking her shoulders loose from his hands. "What the hell difference does it make? McGraw is probably going to kill me now, too."

"Listen," he said fiercely. "That's not going to happen to you. Nothing is going to happen to you. Not as long as I'm around. McGraw or nobody."

"You?" She half-laughed. "You're small game. Just a dumb cowboy that came blundering in. I've tried to tell you that."

"Then tell me straight out," he commanded, his voice fierce. "What the hell is going on around here?"

She studied him a long moment further. It seemed hard for her to bring the words out. Then she said, "They're going to assassinate the President."

He didn't seem to understand. "Do what? Assassinate the President? Who are you talking about? What president?"

"The President of the United States. That's who. The President. General Grant. U. S. Grant. Ever heard of him?"

He still couldn't seem to comprehend the situation and its implications. "I don't understand what you're talking about. The President of the United States? Here?"

"Not here. Of course not here. Listen," she said tensely, "this is all part of a hell of a big scheme. The President is coming down to drive that golden spike, or whatever it is. When the two railroads meet. Don't you know that? McGraw and his gang are going to kill him there, assassinate him there."

He ran a hand over his hair. "Letty, is that true? Are you sure?"

"Sure?" She waved a hand around the room. "What the hell you think this is all about? This private saloon and private cathouse. A place for killers to wait." She laughed bitterly. "All the comforts of home. A little shade for the Sunshine killers, as McGraw says."

He still couldn't seem to take it in. "Letty, give me this slowly. It doesn't make any sense."

"Of course it doesn't make any sense. But it's true."

"But here, in this godforsaken place. Why here?"

"It's just a camp, just a place to wait. They build that track fast or slow. Who can say? But this bunch doesn't leave anything to chance. So they set up this camp here. Just a little south of the line the railroads are taking. And they wait. Wait for the time, for the railroads to meet, for the President to come down and drive that goddam spike. And they don't even care how long they wait because big money is paying them. I mean, big money. That's who wants the job done. And pretty soon they'll move out and do it. So you see, you see what you mean to them? They'll kill you in an instant. You're just some fool blundered into this."

"But why, Letty? What do they want to do that for, assassinate the President?"

She shrugged. "How the hell do I know? I don't even understand it. Something about delaying statehood for some of these western territories. I told you, McGraw is a man who does favors for people. Well, there are people willing to pay him to delay statehood by assassinating the President. Grant got bought off by the wrong money and this money paying McGraw can't move him or something like that. So they got to kill him. And this deal out here with the railroads is the perfect setup. The perfect time. Then you come along and blunder in and kill Ray Tomlain. He was their main gun."

"Letty, how do you know this?"

"I know," she answered. "Some of the men know. Tomlain and Billy and a few of the others. I guess they all know part of it. And they've talked, just enough, drunk, for all of us to know. Even McGraw has talked about it to me. Hell, he don't really care. They've got plans to get out of the country once they've done it with enough money to live like kings the rest of their lives. He's asked me to come with him. Believe it or not. So there you have it. And the only problem they got is what to do with you. Only that ain't really no problem."

He turned away. "I ain't dead yet," he said firmly. "Not by a long shot." There was an old horsehair chair in the corner and he sat down in that and stared at the floor, deep in thought, his face troubled. This had gotten complicated and he didn't like things complicated. He liked them swift and straight, like a rifle bullet. He'd had a quarrel with one man and he'd settled it and now this other which was going to affect him. He wasn't particularly afraid though he was aware that the men conferring in the saloon across the street might be too much for him to handle in the way things were. He didn't know about this President business, this assassination business. The President, the name of the man was nothing more to him than that—a name. For the last few years his home had been the prairies and the mountains of the West, a place the laws and body of the States did not extend to. But he didn't like McGraw, nor any of his gang, nor their methods.

Letty came up and put her hand on his shoulder. "You want a drink?"

He looked up. "No, thanks. Guess not."

"How do you feel?"

"Why, fine. I haven't even thought about it so I guess I'm on the mend. Guess it was that soup you fixed me."

There was a quiet between them for a second and then Letty asked softly, "Who are you, Saulter? Just a hunter?"

He nodded. "Just a hunter."

"Where do you come from?"

He shrugged. "From the South, years ago. Tennessee. But my home's here now. Somewhere out here."

"Were you in the war?"

"Everybody was in the war," he said.

"For the South?"

He nodded.

"Then maybe you don't care what happens to Grant. Maybe you'd just as soon they shot him."

He looked up at her. "I don't care either way," he said. "It's nothing to me. If somebody wants to shoot Grant that's Grant's lookout. Him and his friends."

"You don't care that it's the President?"

He shook his head. "He's just another man to me. He was a pretty good soldier. I expect he can look out for himself."

She nodded her head slowly. "I guess I asked you because I wondered if I was supposed to care. But what the hell does a whore know?"

He frowned. "I wish you wouldn't talk about yourself like that. I don't care how it is you make your living, you're pretty much all right as far as I'm concerned."

"Listen, Saulter . . ." She hesitated. "Listen, I've got an idea what might be going on over there, what they're talking about."

"How so?"

"Well, I bet they're talking about that big rifle of yours. I think Tomlain was supposed to do some rifle shooting in this operation, but of course you've ruined that. There might be a chance they're going to take you in with them. Or offer you the chance."

"I wouldn't do it," he said.

"Oh, goddam!" she swore at him. "If they were going to shoot you if you didn't?"

"All they better do with me is turn me loose."

"Well, they're not going to do that. Look, if they offer you any kind of chance like that you've got to go along with it. Or seem to."

"No."

She raised her fists in exasperation. "Listen, the alternative will be they'll take you out and shoot you."

He shook his head. "A man always has more choices than it seems," he said. "I ain't all that easy to kill. It's been tried before."

"You are the most insane man I've ever seen! Listen, don't turn them down if they offer. For my sake."

He looked up at her quickly. "You worried about McGraw?"

She gave him a disgusted look. "Anything you do ain't going to affect what McGraw does to me. But I'm not scared of McGraw. I can handle him."

At that instant Barney put his head and rifle in the front door. "Mister McGraw is ready for you," he announced. He motioned with the rifle. "Just come on. Slow. No sudden moves."

Saulter got up. He walked halfway across the room and then stopped. He said to Letty, "It'll be all right. Don't worry."

She grimaced. "Sure." Then, as if she couldn't contain herself, she suddenly ran forward and kissed him quickly. Then she turned away and ran out of the room.

SIX

As SAULTER WAS being fetched, Billy was just finishing up his talk with McGraw. They were at one of the tables, a bottle of whiskey between them, empty breakfast dishes pushed to one side. With his clothes still looking as if they'd been hurriedly thrown on, and a light growth of beard on his cheeks, McGraw didn't look so much the polished gentleman. Billy was saying to him, "The point is, Mister McGraw, we got to somehow make good out of what's happened. I know it wasn't supposed to happen, but it has. I feel guilty as hell about it on account of my part, but I can't do anything about that. I just figure we can come out smelling like a rose."

McGraw had grown angrier as the full impact of what had happened had come home. He said coldly, "This job has involved some intense planning. Intense! And a great deal of work on my part and a great deal of money laid out by our bankers."

"I appreciate that, sir," Billy said doggedly, "and I wouldn't have had this happen for the world. But Ray Tomlain is dead and we got this pilgrim on our hands. Maybe this man ain't the rifle shot Tomlain was—I doubt few men are. But he's got the rifle for it and he's got the look. I just got a feeling about him."

"Do you truly expect me to begin making

changes at this late date? I am frankly amazed at you, Billy. I thought you of all these men had a certain amount of intelligence. That's why I've picked you for this job. You ought to understand that you don't make alterations on an undertaking of this magnitude at the eleventh hour. We have been fortunate enough to end up with a ready-made opportunity. We'll not jeopardize it by harebrained fumbling. You were Tomlain's backup. You now become the primary gunner. You'll make the shot."

"But that's just it," Billy said doggedly. "I ain't sure I can make that shot. I can't guarantee it. Ray Tomlain could. He *knew* he could hit first time every time. But I ain't sure. Mister McGraw, that's a shot of nearly a quarter of a mile. I ain't that good. I'm a damn good shot, but I ain't no pluperfect marksman. If Ray Tomlain would have fell over from a fit it would have been all right for me to grab up the rifle and try the shot out of desperation. But it just ain't good thinking to go in with me as your main roper."

McGraw's face was getting tighter and tighter. "You have the reputation. You took the job."

"Yessir, I'm known as a damn good rifle shot. But this one is out of my range. Besides, you got to understand that the rifle we'll be using was Ray's. And for a shot like this you don't just up and begin using a gun, you've got to have *lived* with it. And Ray's been practicing. Every day. And I haven't."

"Goddammit!" McGraw suddenly swore. "I tell you, I can't believe this has happened. I put you down here, kept you down here, where I expected you'd stay out of trouble and be ready at the appointed time. And now look at this mess. You people are idiots. Idiots!"

Billy took a glass and poured himself a half shot of whiskey. He downed it in two swallows. "Well," he finally said, "ain't nothing I can say to that. Except I thought he was doing right. Me and Tomlain was both wrong. But the bad luck was in that old boy being hurt. If that hadn't been the case, we could have persuaded him to go on without too much bother or notice. But you just don't run a wounded man back out in the snow. Least that's what I thought. And I was scared to kill him. Scared who'd come along with questions."

"I still don't understand just what makes you think this man would be as good as Tomlain," McGraw said.

"I've just gotta feeling, Mister McGraw."

"A feeling!"

"No, it's more than that. It's a pretty good hunch. He killed Tomlain in a fair fight. Face to face. That's a bunch. That's a whole bunch. Then he's got that rifle and you take a man like he appears to be and he's got that rifle, that only means one thing. He damn well knows how to use it."

"Have you seen the rifle?"

"Yessir, I took a look at it one morning when we went over to see him and he was still asleep. It's special built. Finest quality I've ever seen. And it is just some kind of cannon! Sonofabitch must be about .90 caliber. No, Mister McGraw, I got my man pegged."

"Hmmm," McGraw said. He dipped the end of his cigar in a glass of whiskey and then put it in his mouth and chewed reflectively.

"What the hell," Billy said. "We can test him out. We still got time for that. Just see if he can shoot. We can kill him any time."

"Which brings up a point."

"Sir?"

"What makes you think he'd cooperate?"

"Huh," Billy said. He gave a short laugh. "Don't seem like much of a choice to me. Put a gun to his head and ask him the question. He'll give the right answer."

"You forget. That has already happened this morning. And he stood there like a statue."

"Yessir. But there was a woman involved. You was askin' him where he'd been and Letty had been hidin' him. Even the worst of us wouldn't talk under them circumstances. Besides, I don't think it's gonna take a gun to his head. You recollect he worked for the railroads, which ought to be good for us since he'll know the layout firsthand. But they run him off and there can't be no love lost over that. I imagine he might be kind of put out with 'em and this ain't exactly gonna be no feather in their cap. He'll see that. Then there's the fact that he's a Southerner. So am I." He stopped and studied a moment, reflecting. "I ain't sure but what I wouldn't shoot Grant for nothin'. I ain't sure but what that's the reason I'm in on this job. Course I'm gonna take the money because I'm gonna need it."

"Well . . ." McGraw said.

"It's worth the chance," Billy urged. "I don't

really reckon it to be much of a chance. Don't trust him. Put a pistol to his head and tell him to hit what you point out. Either he hits it or he gets the bullet."

"Then shoot him anyway," McGraw said, as much to himself as anyone. He blew out a puff of smoke. "All right. Let's get him in here and see what he says. We've got a day or two to kill anyway. This way is as good as any. But—" he added, looking at Billy, "that shot is your responsibility. No matter who makes it. You or him."

Billy nodded. "I understand. I'll get Saulter."

They brought him in and over to the table where McGraw was sitting alone.

McGraw said evenly, "Sit down, Mister Saulter. If that's your name."

Saulter pulled out a chair and eased himself down. Barney sat behind him, the muzzle of his rifle holding steady between his shoulder blades. McGraw pushed the whiskey and a glass across to him. "Help yourself."

Saulter shook his head. "No thanks."

"No? All right." He took a long moment to study the hunter. At length he said, "Tell me about yourself, Mister Saulter. I know a little but you might fill me in a little more."

"Nothing to tell," Saulter said.

"Oh, come now. I'm sure you've had an interesting life. I'm sure you're proud of it, or parts. Tell me about it."

Saulter just stared at him.

McGraw raised his eyebrows. "What, unwilling to talk about yourself? Well, I expect that's all right. I really wasn't interested anyway. I think I know enough already. You don't mind if I have a drink?"

Saulter didn't answer, just watched as McGraw poured himself out a neat ounce of whiskey and tossed if off.

"Now then," he said. He looked around the room. "I'm sure by now you're aware that we're planning a little job. You appear to be that intelligent. What would you say to becoming involved? Taking a part?"

Saulter shifted his gaze from McGraw to the men ranged around the room. "Appears to me you've got enough help."

"Oh, you can never have enough help, Mister Saulter. Especially of the right kind." He paused. "Not to make mention of the deprivation you've caused us of one of our main personnel. I believe you owe us some responsibility of that score."

"Oh, I don't reckon you really think that," Saulter said steadily. "I reckon your man got just about what he was asking for."

McGraw shrugged. "Be that as it may." He poured himself out another tumbler of whiskey. With it almost to his lips, he said, "I understand you've lately left the railroad's employ. As a meat hunter."

Saulter didn't speak.

McGraw set his glass of whiskey down. "Come now, Mister Saulter, I made a simple statement. It is a true one, isn't it?"

Saulter leaned back in his chair and crossed his legs, but didn't reply.

McGraw said, "Mister Saulter, it's going to be

difficult to hold this conversation with you if you won't talk."

Saulter nodded at the killers around the room. "I don't like your audience."

"They're not an audience. They're interested parties. Now, can we establish that you were a hunter for the railroad? That's simple enough."

Saulter shrugged. "You got all the answers."

"And you were cashiered."

"You still got all the answers."

"Yes, but I don't have the why. Will you supply that?"

"Why not, if you're so interested. Though I don't see what it's got to do with the business that's laying between us."

"Let me be the judge of that."

"I shot a couple of men," Saulter said.

McGraw lifted his eyebrows. "That seems to be a habit of yours. Was it a fair fight?"

Saulter shrugged. "Fair if you think two of them coming at me is fair."

McGraw smiled. "Well put, sir. But if it was fair, why were you fired?"

Saulter looked at McGraw. Then he took a moment to get out one of the little black cigars from his pocket. He deliberately scratched a match on his boot heel and took a long time lighting the smoke. Then he shook the match out and flipped it up on the table. He said, "You're damn curious about a lot of things."

"You ought to be grateful for that, Mister Saulter. If I wasn't you'd have already been shot."

Saulter said abruptly. "The boss said he couldn't afford no chance of trouble. Not then."

"Why was that?"

"Said we was nearing completion and there'd be ceremonies and officials around. Said I might bring on trouble from these men's friends. That suit you?"

McGraw nodded, a pleased look on his face. He sat back in his chair and studied the hunter for a long moment. "You're in a pretty tight fix, Saulter. Have you considered that?"

Saulter didn't answer. There was none for such a question.

"You don't seem too concerned that I might have you shot in the next five minutes."

"I'll get concerned," Saulter said, "at the right time."

"But now is not the right time?"

"Doesn't appear to be."

"Why not?"

"You're talking. You want something. If you were going to shoot me you wouldn't waste all this breath."

"What is it you think I want?"

"I don't know."

McGraw leaned forward intently. "I have heard about your big rifle. Are you good with it? Can you use it?"

A small smile came to Saulter's mouth.

"I mean, are you really expert? What could you hit at four hundred yards? Could you hit a top hat?"

The smile stayed on Saulter's lips.

"A playing card?"

"There's one way to find out," Saulter said.

"And what would that be?"

"Give me the rifle and get off four hundred yards and put the card in your breast pocket."

McGraw laughed dryly. "Your sense of humor impresses me."

Saulter nodded, but didn't speak.

McGraw looked over at Billy. He said to the gunman, "You may be right." Then he switched back to Saulter. "I'm putting this to you seriously. How would you like to cooperate with us in the matter we have at hand? You would first have to prove your ability at long-range marksmanship, but you seem obviously sure of yourself there. But once satisfied, I could offer you the opportunity to even up your score with the railroad and make yourself a very handsome payday at the same time."

"No," Saulter said distinctly.

McGraw looked faintly surprised. "No? Just like that? Knowing no more about the job, you say no?"

"I don't like you," Saulter said, "and I don't like your crowd. I don't have to know much about your work to know I don't want any part of it." His face was impassive, giving away nothing of what he was thinking. Only the faint movement of his eyes as they flicked about the room showed that he was tensing up for the trouble he felt was very near.

McGraw laughed, a short ugly bark. "That's the most absurd remark I've ever heard." He leaned toward Saulter. "You're not in a position to give in to your likes and dislikes, *Mister* Saulter. Has it occurred to you, you might not have a choice?"

"Oh," Saulter said easily, "a man always has a choice."

"A fool maybe," McGraw said. "Now let me tell you something. And let me put it so you don't misunderstand for apparently you don't have the brains I gave you credit for. You are either going to ride out of here when we do, point that big gun at what I tell you to, pull the trigger when I tell you, and hit what I tell you, or else I'll have you shot. Is that clear? I'll have you shot dead."

Saulter didn't reply.

"And further understand this," McGraw said angrily, "I haven't decided to take you in. I am offering you the chance to convince me I should. And at this point that might take some doing. You'll have to show me you're very expert with that rifle. And very trustworthy."

"No," Saulter said flatly.

"Then I'll shoot you," McGraw said. "Barney, William! Take this fool over to the bunkhouse and set him down and let him think. Keep him under close guard. No mistakes." He took out his gold watch, snapped it open, and laid it on the table. "You've got exactly half an hour to make up your mind. Thirty minutes." McGraw was very angry. "And by god, sir, you'd better come back in here talking like a straw lawyer, begging for a chance, or I give you my word I'll have you shot within sixty seconds. Now get him out of here."

They prodded Saulter up from his chair and out the door with their rifles. They watched until he'd disappeared and then Billy asked, "You think he'll come around, Mister McGraw?"

McGraw said angrily, "I don't give a damn if he

does or not. It would give me great pleasure to shoot the arrogant bastard. Who the hell does he think he is?"

"Well, I don't care one way or another about shooting him. But if we need him . . ."

"I really don't know," McGraw said. "If he's good enough with that rifle we've got to use him. There's too much at stake. Then I'll shoot him. If he comes around."

Billy said, "I know a way to make him agree."

"How? He's got a gun at his head now."

"Not his head, Letty's."

"A whore he doesn't even know? I don't believe it."

"Yessir. I know Mister Saulter and his kind. I grew up working on plantations of them proud, honorable bastards. They got this code about women and all women has got to be treated the same. You put a gun to Letty's head and he'll do whatever you tell him. You seen how he was this morning."

McGraw looked at him. "By god, you may be right. We'll hold that in reserve."

Across the way Letty had come out on the porch. Shielding her eyes against the glare she watched as Saulter was taken across to the bunkhouse. She waited until they had disappeared inside and then abruptly whirled around and went back in the house. Quickly she crossed the living room to the rough bar, located a bottle of whiskey and a glass, paused to put on a long cape, and then slipped out the back door. She circled wide around her own barn, crossed the road well down from

the saloon, and made her way toward the door at
the far end of the bunkhouse.

Inside Saulter was sitting on one of the bunks
with Barney and William, both covering him with
their rifles, sitting on another bunk facing him.
Barney asked, "Would you care for a smoke?"

"Thanks," Saulter said. He took the cigar Barney proffered, lit it, and sat there studying the two
through a cloud of blue smoke.

Saulter's unflinching gaze made Barney nervous. He said, "Instead of sittin' there feelin'
pleased with yourself for being so smart ass with
the Captain you ought to get to makin' your mind
up. Or sayin' your prayers. Cause I can tell you
that Mister McGraw don't fool around. You don't
go pussy-footin' in there with the right answers
and you'll sure as hell be dead in exactly sixty
seconds. I tell you, you better see the straight of
this matter. The way the Captain wants you to."

Saulter smiled thinly but didn't speak.

It made Barney more nervous. "You're a cool
one, ain't'cha? Well, don't get no ideas about
jumpin' around. I bet it'd suit Mister McGraw if
we just up and plugged you here and now. Ain't
that right, Will? Save him the trouble of listening
to you whinny around and beg."

"Take it easy," Saulter said.

"Brother, you're the one better take it easy,"
Williams said. "I wouldn't want to be in your
boots."

Saulter smiled thinly. "I thought it was my
choice."

"I expect it is," Barney answered. "But you'd be

a lot better off if you'd been civil with the Captain in there. The Captain's a big man and he don't take nothin' off some saddle tramp."

William, at that point, took a pocket watch out, and looked at it. "I make it to be fifteen minutes passed. We have him in there at the half hour sharp."

"Now," Barney said, "you make up your mind to go back there and be respectful to the Captain and he'll give you a fair shake. Hell, he's offerin' you a chance on a mighty big job. Plenty gunners'd give a gallon of blood to get in on this. Hell, man."

Saulter asked softly, "Do you know what the job is?"

Barney said, "Not exactly. I know it involves them railroads. And I know we got to plug some hombres. That's enough for me to know."

William said, "You better cut out the claptrap, Barney."

"I ain't told him nothin'."

Saulter looked at both of them, the thin smile on his face, his eyes narrowed.

Then the back door of the bunkhouse opened and Letty came in carrying the whiskey. Barney and William raised their rifles, but they lowered them as they recognized Letty.

Saulter shifted just enough to see that it was Letty. She came forward as Barney, smiling, said, "Why, look here, it's Miss Pretty."

"Letty, I don't reckon you ought to be in here," Will cut in.

She didn't need him. "Oh, I'm not staying," she said, looking at Saulter. "I just brought Mister Saulter a little whiskey. I got a feeling he's going to need it." Her voice was hard, bitter. Saulter glanced up at her but there was nothing in her face.

Barney cackled, but Will was frowning. "I don't know . . ."

But Letty was already pouring a glass. It was a large glass and she poured it full. "Here," she said, thrusting it at Saulter. He took it, looking at her, as she backed away a step or two.

For a moment Saulter held the glass, motionless. He started to raise it to his lips and then seemed to notice Barney. With a half grin he held it out. "You first, you might have to shoot me. I want your hand steady."

Barney cackled at the joke. He shifted his rifle, the muzzle now pointing toward the ceiling, and reached to take the glass. As he did Saulter suddenly threw it sideways in William's face, the raw whiskey blinding him. Almost in the same motion Saulter's other hand flashed out and jerked the rifle out of Barney's hand. He grabbed it by the barrel and, without a lost motion, brought it crashing down on William's head, the impact splintering the stock. William rolled off the bunk. Wheeling, Saulter hit Barney across the face with the remainder of the rifle and then kicked him in the head as he fell sideways. He whirled, not an instant lost, and grabbing Letty by the arm, went running for the back door of the bunkhouse, dragging her along behind him. They shot out the door and turned toward the women's house. As they crossed the road he slowed and pulled her up to him. "Get in that house and stay there. Don't go in that saloon no matter what!"

"Where are you going?" she cried. "What are you going to do?"

"Fight," he said.

"You need a gun."

"I've got a gun," he said. He pushed her toward the house and then took off at a dead run for the barn. She watched him a second and then hurried into the house.

Saulter dashed into the barn and ran for his horse. Catching up the reins he vaulted into the saddle. The big front doors stood open and he dashed through, into the clear. At the road he cut right, already drawing out his big rifle as he spotted his horse out of the little town.

In the saloon they had seen or heard nothing. McGraw and Billy were still sitting at the table drinking whiskey. McGraw picked his watch up and looked at it. "Three minutes," he said. He smiled, not humorously. "I wonder what our southern gentleman has decided."

"What about Letty?" Billy asked. "Hadn't we ought to get her over here?"

McGraw turned to one of the other men. "Runt, step over to the women's house and escort Miss Letty over here. Do not be rough with her."

"Yessir," the man said. He shrugged into a coat and opened the door and stepped out on the porch. At that instant Saulter came charging by, spurring his horse into a hard run as he headed for the high land a half mile out of town. The man stared, then reacted, his hand instinctively reaching for his side gun. But the long coat he was wearing hampered his draw and Saulter was out of range before he could clear his weapon. He whirled and dashed back into the saloon. "He's got away," he yelled. "That Saulter. He's ridin' out of town."

"Goddammit." McGraw jumped to his feet, cursing, his face livid. "After him! Catch him! Move, goddammit!"

Billy yelled to the other men, "Get the horses." They all went scrambling for the back door, bunching up at the entrance, scrambling and tripping in their haste. Because of the weather all the horses were kept in the barn behind the saloon. It was fifty yards away, across a clear expanse of snow. In a pack they came charging out the back door, heading for the barn. At that instant Barney and William came staggering out of the bunkhouse. Both of their faces were a mass of blood. Barney was still so groggy he was stumbling. He fell just as he came out the door but immediately got up. All the time he was yelling, "Help! Help! Help!"

The gang of men slowed and stopped. Billy ran a few steps in that direction. "What the hell happened?"

"I don't know," Barney moaned, his hands to his face. "He kicked the hell out of me. I'm damn near blind." He stumbled and fell in the deep snow.

"Let's get the horses," Billy said.

They started running again. Halfway to the barn there was a sudden huge boom and one of the gunmen went cartwheeling sideways. He skidded to a stop in the snow with blood pumping out a huge hole.

The gunmen instinctively looked in the direction of the shot. On top of a low hill, Saulter was silhouetted against the sky. He was sitting on his buffalo horse, rapidly working the action to reload.

"Goddammit!" Billy yelled. "He's got that big gun. Hit for cover."

They scattered; Billy and William and another gunman broke back for the saloon. Two others, thinking it was closer, ran for the barn. Another shot boomed out and kicked up a spray of snow at Billy's feet. But in another second they all had reached cover except Barney, who was wandering around yelling for help. Then there was another shot and he went flipping over backwards.

On the little hill, Saulter sat on his horse and slowly ejected the spent shell. He put the hull in his pocket, drew out a fresh shell, and reloaded. His face was grim and impassive. With a gentle nudge he put his horse into a canter, riding around the crest of the little circling hills to take up the attack from a fresh quarter.

In the saloon Billy and William were reporting to Mister McGraw. They were all crunched down below the front window, trying to see out. Billy and William were panting from their run. Saulter had hit William over one eye with the rifle butt, inflicting a deep cut, and the blood was still cascading down, half blinding him. He was trying, unsuccessfully, to keep it wiped away with a bandanna handkerchief. Finally he just tied it around his forehead like a headband.

Billy said briefly, "Clemson and Runt are in the barn. Barney and Ellis are dead."

McGraw was not in a rage. His feelings were somewhere between surprise and demonic frustration. But, at Billy's words that two more of his carefully recruited team were now useless to him, his color suddenly heightened and he screamed at William, "You fool! You idiotic fools! Do you realize what this means?" He suddenly reached out and grabbed the gunman by the collar. "How did the man get away from you? You were holding guns on him! Explain to me how this could happen!" He was shouting by the time he finished, shouting and jerking William back and forth like he was shaking a child.

"It was Letty," William said. He made no attempt to break loose from McGraw's grip. "She come in and give Saulter a glass of whiskey and he threw it in my face. Then he got Barney's rifle and clubbed me down with it. I didn't see what he done to Barney."

Now true rage broke through what was left of McGraw's composure. He was so angry he was shaking. "That bitch!" he screamed. "I'll cut the tits off that traitorous sow. I'll slit her nose. I'll open her belly and fill it with dirt!" He looked wildly around. "Where is she? Is she in this room?" He stood up and drew out his pistol. Billy was tugging at his coat, trying to pull him down.

"You better get away from the window," Billy said. "He's out there."

McGraw disregarded him, but then there came a far-off boom and a huge shell came whistling through the room and thudded into the floor. Debris and pieces of ceiling came falling down. McGraw instantly fell prostrate, the anger in his face replaced with sudden fear.

Billy looked up. A hole a foot and a half across

had appeared in the exposed roof. "My god," Billy said shakily, "that thing's a cannon!"

At the shot, Schmidt, who had been standing in the middle of the room reacting with dazed astonishment at what was happening, suddenly raced a few lumbering steps and dived behind the bar. He stuck his head up and yelled at McGraw, "I didn't bargain for this!"

"Shut up, fool!" McGraw yelled. In his frustration and rage he snapped off a quick shot at the saloon keeper. It went wild but Schmidt dropped instantly out of sight again.

Across the room Chiffon was in his accustomed place by the fireplace. But now he was curled into a tight ball, clinging to the side of the fireplace and whimpering, "Eeeeh, eeeh, eeeh," over and over.

The other gunman was at the back door, peering out, trying to locate Saulter.

In the quiet that had come another shot suddenly boomed out and instantly pieces of the ceiling began to fall. Billy swore quietly and intensely.

With the new silence after that shot the gunman at the back door quickly scuttled across the floor and came up to the group at the window. "What the hell are we going to do, Mister McGraw?"

"I don't know," McGraw said. He was huddled down below the window, hugging the wall. "You fools have allowed this mess."

Billy said, "Just stay out of the middle of the room. Big as that gun of his is it can't shoot through the walls."

"Yeah, but what are we going to do about that hombre out there? He's got us bottled up tight."

William was peering over the ledge of the window, searching the horizon. "Yonder he is," he said. "Up there on top of the ridge just to the left of the women's house."

They all risked a look sticking their heads up gingerly as if they expected a shot at any instant. Saulter was clearly visible, outlined against the brilliantly blue sky, on top of a hummock a full half mile distant. As they watched a puff of black smoke suddenly clouded his figure and a bullet came whistling through the top of the window, shattering sash and wooden shutters. They ducked instinctively, even though the bullet was already past. A shower of wood and plaster fell down on their shoulders.

"Well," Billy said dryly, "we know now that a four-hundred-yard shot wouldn't have been shucks for him."

In the knowledge that it would take him a few seconds to reload they again peered over the ledge. Saulter was where he was before. They could see him deliberately breaking down his rifle and inserting another shell. McGraw said in a voice a pitch too high for normal, "Shoot him! Somebody shoot him!" A new emotion was mixing in with his rage: fear.

It was not yet fear for his life, but was more a shocked realization that all of his carefully laid plans were somehow going awry. It had not come fully home to him yet because he couldn't conceive how one man could dismantle preparations that had taken months and countless sums of money. Even in the ludicrous position he suddenly found himself occupying, he still clung to the impregnable protection of the money he represented as proof against almost anything. It had always been that way in the past and it was not now part of his subconscious thinking to feel otherwise. But panic was beginning to edge into his normally ordered mind. He demanded again, "Shoot him, I say!"

"It's too far, Mister McGraw. He's out of range. That cannon of his must carry a mile."

"This is pitiful!" McGraw said viciously. "I supposedly hired the best gunmen in the country and they can't handle one meat hunter! Here we are, pinned down like rabbits!"

The gun boomed out again and the top half of the window disappeared. They ducked quickly behind the protecting ledge amid a shower of glass. Billy muttered, "I told Tomlain to leave that fellow alone. I told him!"

McGraw snarled, "You should have killed him." He took a cautious peek above the ledge. "We've got to get him."

"How, Mister McGraw?"

"Rush him."

Billy shuddered. "That'd be suicide. He'd pick us off before we got within a hundred yards. We'd never even get to the horses."

McGraw looked around calculating. William pointed to Chiffo. "How about that half-breed yonder? We could send him to bring the horses."

"Do it," McGraw ordered.

Running crouched, as if under open fire, William dashed across the room and pulled Chiffo to his feet. Roughly he shoved him along to the back door. "Got an errand for you, boy."

"I don't go, Meester. I scairt."

"You'll be dead, you ain't damned quick," William said brutally. He jerked the door open. "You run yonder to that barn and tell them two men to get over here with horses. You got that?"

"I don't go."

"You go," William said. He put his pistol to Chiffo's head. "Tell 'em to shelter behind this building. Now git!" He shoved Chiffo through the door.

The boy took off running, but instead of heading for the barn, he turned for the bunkhouse. William swore. "That little sonofabitch!" He aimed his revolver and fired two shots quickly. One went wild, but one caught Chiffo in the calf of one leg and he went spinning into the snow, five yards short of the bunkhouse door. Seeing he'd only wounded the boy, William fired again, but Chiffo was up, like a three-legged cat, scuttling for the door. A bullet hit the door near his head, but in another instant, he was inside.

William turned back to the front, standing erect. "Goddam, Mister McGraw, what do we do now?"

But, before McGraw could answer, Saulter's rifle boomed and William suddenly screamed and went down, his legs cut out from under him as if by a giant hand. He was hit in the upper thigh, but the hole was such that it didn't matter that it wasn't in a vital spot.

Billy started toward him, but again the huge rifle boomed and more of the ceiling fell down.

Billy ducked back and yelled for Schmidt to drag William to cover. The saloon keeper grumbled, but he reached out and got William by the collar and dragged him behind the rough bar.

Billy asked, "Now what?"

McGraw, looking worried said, "Crawl to the door. See if they can hear you in the barn."

Up on the slopes, Saulter had changed his position again. He'd ridden around to where the hills broke for the little road that led into the town. Looking at the settlement, he could see the door of the barn open cautiously. Quickly he raised his rifle and fired. Splinters flew from the barn door and it was quickly shut.

Over in the women's house Letty and the others were in the front room looking out the windows. They instinctively flinched as Saulter's rifle boomed out. One of them asked Letty what they should do.

"Do?" Letty looked around at her in annoyance. "What the hell are you talking about? We sit and wait." Under her breath she said lowly, "But you better damn well pray that Saulter wins."

The inside of the saloon was beginning to disintegrate. There was debris all over the floor from the damaged roof and the blown out windows. Some of the bullets did not plow directly into the floor but instead hit it at such an angle that they glanced off and ricocheted wildly before finally embedding themselves in the plaster walls. Billy had turned over one of the heavy tables and pulled it over behind McGraw, him and the other gunman as protection against the ricochets. He called across the bar to Schmidt, "How's William? He holding on?"

Schmidt said from behind the bar. "He's gonna die pretty damn quick. His face is all white."

"Can't you do something?" Billy called back. "Can't you put a tourniquet on his leg or something?"

Schmidt gave a shrug. "Wouldn't do no damn good. You ought to see all this blood on the floor. He ain't got none left to keep in him."

Billy turned to McGraw. "This is getting out of hand. We got to do something. We stay pinned up in here and he's going to pick us off like a turkey shoot."

The panic stronger in his voice, McGraw said, "We've got to get him quick. Before he can destroy our plans."

"Plans?" Billy looked doubtful. "I just want out of here alive. Mister McGraw, they ain't but five of us left, counting you."

McGraw looked at him, blinking rapidly. "Five? Five men is all?"

"Yessir. He's killed four. If William is dead."

"This is not possible!" McGraw said. "It is not possible. I don't understand what has happened."

At the head of the street Saulter had decided on a more direct course of action. He all of a sudden spurred his horse to a run and came cutting up the road. Just before he got to the saloon he slipped over the side of the saddle. He had his right leg hooked over the top of the horse's rump, while his left leg was wrapped around underneath the horse's neck. With his left arm he held the saddle horn and the end of his rifle. He had his rifle laid across the saddle in a firing position. He came dashing by the saloon. As he passed, he fired, hitting the door at the latch. The huge bullet burst the lock and blew the door half off its hinges.

Inside, the men jumped as the door came flying open.

"Mein Gott!" Schmidt yelled.

McGraw said, "Get back there and signal for them to bring the horses. We've got to get out of here."

Billy crawled rapidly to the back door. Yelling and firing his pistol he was able to attract the attention of one of the men who stuck his head cautiously out the barn door.

"Bring horses!" Billy yelled. "And come."

"Now?" The man looked frightened.

"Yes," Billy called back.

At that moment Saulter came dashing back the other way. Again his rifle boomed and a huge shell crashed into the door, this time completely carrying it away. It fell in a shower of splinters and Billy instinctively jumped sideways. Then he got up and sprinted back to the window.

"He's going to be in here in a minute."

McGraw was beginning to look frightened. "A quarter of a million dollars," he said. "A quarter of a million dollars! Money!"

"What quarter of a million dollars?"

McGraw turned savagely on him. "That's what this job is worth. And this gun tramp is ruining it. Goddammit, we've got to kill him quick." He whirled, looking wildly around. "What is holding

up those men? Billy, get to the back door and look
for them."

Billy crawled cautiously to the door. Another
shot boomed out and the bottles behind the bar
suddenly exploded.

"I am shot!" Schmidt screamed. He raised up,
blood streaming down his face from cuts from the
flying glass. He yelled at McGraw, "You get out!
You hear? You get out right now!" McGraw
whirled and snapped off another shot at him, but
it too missed as he disappeared down behind the
bar.

Billy called. "They about ready. They got the
barn door open."

Saulter had ridden on around the little circle of
hills until his position was slightly behind the
saloon. But he was still far enough toward the
front that he could see the front of the barn.
He saw the doors swing open and knew instinctively what was happening. "Not likely," he said
half aloud. He was reloading and he completed
the work quickly and then took another shell
from his satchel and stuck it in his mouth like a
brass cigar, anticipating the need for fast work.
Then he saw a figure at the back door of the
saloon, signaling to the men in the barn. It would
be an easy shot and he quickly raised his rifle. But
over his sights something about the vague figure
made him recognize Billy, and he slowly lowered
his rifle. "All right. That makes us even," he
muttered to himself.

He switched his attention to the barn. He had
his rifle up and was ready when the two gunmen
hidden there suddenly came bursting out on

horseback. They had two other horses in lead. It was only fifty yards to the saloon, but they had the horses at a dead run, riding low in the saddle and quirting and slashing at their mounts. Saulter took aim on the lead man and fired, the rifle pounding back into his shoulder with that heavy recoil few men could have withstood for long. The shot missed the man, but hit the horse, and animal and man went down in a tangle. The other rider swept on by, heading for the back of the saloon. Saulter reloaded quickly. In the pause the downed rider had made it to his feet and was sprinting for the door. Saulter got his sights on him and followed along, letting him get almost to the door before he fired. The shell caught the man squarely in the back and catapulted him through the opening. Its force was such that he skidded halfway across the floor. He came to rest only a few feet from McGraw.

McGraw stared aghast at the figure on the floor. Blood briefly pulsed a foot high out of the dead back and then subsided into a rapidly growing pool on the floor.

The other man had made it safely to shelter and he came racing through the door and threw himself down beside McGraw. "We're in a storm!" he cried.

Billy suddenly broke from the door and raced to the group under the window. "Two of the horses got away. You didn't tie them good." He looked at the man who had survived the ride from the barn.

"You goddam right!" the man shouted at him. "Like to see you standin' there tyin' square knots with that fucking artillery blasting away at you!"

"Point is," Billy said, "they ain't but two horses now. Two got away and Saulter shot one." He ducked as another shot whistled through the roof. "But personally, somebody can have mine. I don't think we'd get a hundred yards before that man picked us off. I saw him get Runt at a dead run and he's got to be six hundred yards away." He looked over at the dead man in the middle of the floor. "We're in real trouble, Mister McGraw."

"I can see that!" McGraw snapped wildly. His cool air of aloof command had completely disintegrated now. His every word was high and frightened.

"Job's done for, anyway."

"I'll decide that," McGraw snapped shrilly.

"Just us four now," Billy said. "Wonder if that man would accept a surrender. Unconditional."

"Shut your mouth!"

McGraw raised his head to peer cautiously out over the window ledge, forgetting that the shots were now coming from the rear. Saulter reminded him of his position with a shot that tore the back door loose from its hinges. In a moment there was another shot and the door fell to the floor.

"McGraw," Billy said urgently, for the first time neglecting to use the Mr., "we got to get out of here. He's going to shoot this damn place down!"

Even as he spoke vagrant afternoon winds began to whip drift snow through both open doors and through the holes in the roof. It spread slowly across the floor in a thin layer. And the fire, which had been untended for some time, had died down so that the cold was entering steadily.

The gunman who'd brought the horses said, "I wisht it was dark. We could make a break then. How long ya figure?"

Billy said, "Two hours at least."

McGraw asked tensely, "Anyone know where he is now?"

Saulter had come back around to the front of the saloon. He sat on his horse and studied the place. Then he too glanced up at the sky, estimating the sun's position and how much time he had before nightfall. He sat there wishing he knew how many of them there were left. He could only count on three for sure, four counting Tomlain. That left five of them, including McGraw, but not including Schmidt. But he felt—he had to believe—that he'd done some damage with the blind shots he'd been firing through the roof. There would be ricochets off the oaken floor and the plaster walls and ricochets had to eventually hit someone. Resting, he noticed how tired he was and how he ached and hurt. He had fired his big rifle more and faster than ever before in such a short span of time, and his shoulder had taken a terrific pounding. It was taking all his will and determination now not to instinctively flinch when he pulled the trigger. He didn't know how many more times he could fire it. And his side was hurting him. It was healing and he no longer felt that sick weakness, but the wrenching he'd given it with the riding and the shooting had moved the ends of his broken ribs around and they stabbed him afresh with each new movement.

He was worried about night coming on. If he

hadn't finished them off by dark he might be in trouble. He had to keep them bottled up, not allow them to scatter, for once they did he'd no longer be in control. He would have to spend the night in the women's house, for he couldn't survive outside in the cold, but if he did that they would know it by morning and then he'd be the one surrounded. He could just ride away, but he had no intention of leaving Letty, not so long as there was one assassin left alive or unfettered.

So he sat there trying to think of some plan to determine what he was still facing. Everyone might be dead for all he knew.

In the saloon Billy raised his head up cautiously and peered out. He located Saulter on the little hummock. "He's back around on our side. Just out in front and a little around to the left." He watched another moment and then said urgently, "Get down! He's fixing to fire."

There was a loud boom and then another bullet came through the roof. They heard it strike the front of the fireplace and come singing off the rock. Then the gunman who'd brought the horses suddenly said, "Ohhh!" and fell over, the back of his head gone. Blood sprayed out and McGraw caught some of the mist on his white shirt front. He looked down at it in dismay and then quickly drew away from the spreading puddle on the floor.

"Well, that's three," Billy said matter-of-factly. "Me, you, and Jackhammer. And if you want to talk about gunhands that leaves two. Me and Jack." He looked at McGraw. "I seen you shoot at Schmidt twice and you ain't even hit that fat sonofabitch."

"Shut up," McGraw said automatically.

"I will," Billy said, "if you'll think of something for us to do. You're supposed to be the boss."

McGraw said, "I think we're going to surrender."

Jackhammer said, "Bullshit."

Billy said, "Good luck."

"Billy," McGraw said tensely.

"Sir?"

"Take this." McGraw pulled out a large white handkerchief. He handed it to Billy. "Take that out there and wave it at him. Tell him you surrender."

Billy shook his head. "Not very damn likely."

"Do what I say!"

"No thank you. I don't think our Mister Saulter would accept a surrender."

"We're not going to surrender, you fool. I just want you to draw him down here in rifle shot. Now take this handkerchief and go on. We'll have him covered."

But Billy shook his head. "He'll shoot me down minute I go out that door."

"No he won't," McGraw insisted. "He's a gentleman."

"Yes, and he's been pushed about as far as he'll go. He ain't going to fall for something like that, anyway."

"Tell him you're the only one left. That everyone else is dead. Tell him you want to surrender. You just have to draw him a little closer. He's almost in rifle range now."

"McGraw, I tell you he ain't going to fall for it.

He's smart." Billy raised his head cautiously to take another look at Saulter. He was in the same place, some six hundred yards away, just sitting on his horse. As Billy watched, Saulter raised his rifle and fired again. More of the ceiling came down and the ricochet wound around and buried itself in the wall post a foot to their right.

The third man said, "He's going to freeze us out if nothing else."

Billy said, "Why should he come down? He'll make me come up."

McGraw thought for a moment. Finally he turned and slid to where the dead gunman lay. McGraw, with an effort, tore the back out of his blood-soaked shirt. He worked his way back over to Billy and rubbed the blood on Billy's pants leg. Billy jerked away. "Here, what are you doing?"

"Hold still," McGraw ordered. He finished rubbing the blood on. "Limp when you go out. Tell him you're wounded."

Billy said, "You're crazy. It won't work."

"Start up toward him and then fall down. Act like you can't walk. He'll have to come down. Just a hundred yards and we've got him."

"I'm not going to do it," Billy said. "He'll shoot me on sight."

"I'll give you two hundred dollars."

"No," Billy said.

McGraw looked at him steadily. "I'll give you five hundred."

Billy was uncertain. "Five hundred?"

Jackhammer said, "Hell, I'll do it for that, Mister McGraw."

But McGraw went on looking at Billy. "No, I

think he'll be more friendly with Billy. He knows he talked up for him. Saved his skin. Didn't you, Billy?"

"It seemed like the right thing at the time," Billy said, looking down.

"Five hundred."

"Cash?"

"Yes."

"Give it to me."

"It's over in the women's house. I'll pay you as soon as we're rid of Saulter. Well? We wouldn't be in this fix if it weren't for you."

"Oh hell," Billy said in resignation. He rolled to his hands and knees. "Gimme that handkerchief."

Holding the handkerchief in one hand and his rifle in the other he crawled along the wall to the door. Looking back over his shoulder he said, "Just you don't forget you owe me that five hundred. And you make sure before you fire." He turned back to the door. Cautiously he stuck his head in the opening, frantically signaling with the handkerchief.

Up on the knoll, Saulter straightened in the saddle. His eyes narrowed as he studied the surrender flag. He raised his rifle.

Cautiously, Billy slowly eased out in the door, desperately waving the handkerchief. He raised himself in the doorway, calling out, "Don't shoot! Don't shoot!"

Saulter peered down the sights of his rifle at him. Billy took a hesitant step out on the porch. He had both hands over his head, the handkerchief in one, his rifle in the other. He took another step, faking the limp, and threw his rifle out in the snow. Before moving, he called back to the door, in a hoarse whisper, "Don't you shoot till you're sure. You hear? Don't you miss him!"

He took another limping, hesitant step forward. Looking up at Saulter he called, "I surrender. They're all dead. And I'm wounded."

Saulter didn't answer. Just stared at him over the sights of his rifle.

Billy kept coming one slow step and then another. "I can't walk!" he called. "You've nearly blowed my leg off."

Letty was peering through the curtains of the house at the little drama. "What the hell? Look there, Flora, can you see a head behind that window? Look close."

Carefully, faking the limp very effectively, Billy stepped down off the porch. He took two steps out in the snow, waving his flag. "Saulter! Help me! I'm bleedin' to death." He walked a few more steps then appeared to stagger. Clutching at his leg, the one with the blood smeared on it, he suddenly pitched forward in the snow. Saulter slowly lowered his rifle. Billy rolled over, clutching his leg, waving his surrender flag. "Saulter! Help me!" He made as if to rise, struggling up on his mock wounded leg, and then collapsed back in the snow. He was sure now Saulter wasn't going to shoot him. "Please," he called, "please, for god's sake! I'm all that's left. You've wiped us out!"

In the saloon McGraw was peering over the ledge, just at the corner of the window.

The other gunman asked tensely, "He coming yet?"

"Not yet," McGraw said. "But he looks like he's going to. He's not going to shoot."

The gunman said, "Listen to old Billy, would you? Boy, he's really playactin'. I'd never knowed he had it in him."

McGraw said sharply, "Be ready with your rifle. He could come at any second."

"I'm ready," the man vowed. "Just one shot at that sonofabitch."

"But you don't fire until I give you the word," McGraw ordered, still peering out intently at the corner of the window. "You must not miss!"

Saulter sat there staring thoughtfully at the figure in the snow. The safe thing would be just to pump a bullet into the man and wait. If there were anymore left they'd have to make a move sooner or later. But he hated to shoot Billy. No matter what he was or who he was in with, the man had gone to the well several times for him. And he did look hurt and act hurt. He could see the blood very distinctly against the gray of his breeches. And more, Billy just didn't seem like the kind of man who could play such a sham trick. It all made sense; there hadn't been a sound out of them for some time now.

He looked up at the sun, noticing how much lower it was in the sky. It would be dark in not too long and the sky was taking on that leaden look that meant more snow. He made up his mind and decided he would go down, cautiously, and have a look. Perhaps it was all over. He would be very relieved if that was so. He was tired and hurting and cold. He thought of Letty. It would be nice to be with her in that house, drinking whiskey and lying in bed together. He put his spurs lightly to his horse, urging the animal ahead slowly.

McGraw said, tightly, "He's coming!"

"One shot," Jackhammer mumbled, "just one shot."

"We want him close," McGraw ordered. "Don't you jump the gun." With the chance to finally close with his enemy, McGraw was regaining some of his composure.

Saulter came on, picking his way hesitantly. He was fifty yards closer. Another one hundred and he'd be in reasonable range for the type of rifles Jackhammer and McGraw had.

In the saloon McGraw slowly came to his knees, his rifle at the ready. On the other side of the window Jackhammer was also ready.

Billy lay in the snow, calling over and over. "Help! Saulter, I'm bleeding to death. Help me!"

With a little over three hundred yards to go Saulter pulled his horse up and studied the façade of the saloon. Then he looked left and then right. The only sign of life was Billy laying in the snow waving his surrender flag.

"He's stopped, goddammit!" McGraw gritted out through his teeth.

"I could try a shot," Jackhammer said. "Might have a chance."

"No! As soon as you put your rifle through the window he'd see it and break. Maybe—he's moving again." He edged his face around the sill further to see Saulter better, now going down and coming up a small hummock. "Just a little further. At a hundred yards we'll have time for several shots."

On Saulter came, riding slowly, his eyes sweeping the terrain in front of him. He was within two hundred yards.

Letty had her face pressed against the windowpane. She was almost certain she could make out some dark shadow at the corner of the saloon window. She suddenly made up her mind. "Goddammit, it's a trap."

She whirled and dashed for the back door. Saulter was still beyond the women's house, from the saloon, and about fifty yards to one side. Letty was yelling at him as she hit the snow. "Saulter! Look out! It's a trap, they're laying for you." She sprinted toward him, having heavy going in the deep snow.

He swung in the saddle, startled, looking toward her. He could tell she was agitated by the way she was waving her arms, but the wind was against her and he couldn't make out the words she was yelling. But then she broke past the end of the house and McGraw was able to see her from the saloon. He let out a string of curses. "Fire, fire!" he yelled at Jackhammer. "Shoot him!"

At that moment, Saulter made out one word Letty was yelling: ". . . trap!" He instinctively reined his horse back hard. The animal came up, wheeling and rearing. It was at that moment that they began firing from the saloon, but the horse, up on his hind legs, was hiding Saulter with his body. In the saddle Saulter could feel and hear the shells hitting his horse. He felt the animal falter, stumble, and still on his hind legs, begin to fall. He timed his leap, kicking loose from the stirrups and jumping free just before the animal hit the ground. He landed behind the animal and, without pause, wiggled up to the shivering carcass and threw his rifle down in firing position. He saw that Letty had already thrown herself facedown in the snow. "Stay down!" he yelled at her.

At his words, Billy, who realized they'd missed, suddenly jumped to his feet and broke for the saloon. He hit the porch, skidded on the slick snow, and lost his balance. As he whirled to his feet, Saulter fired. Billy was almost facing back the way he'd come by the time the bullet took him. It hit him in the left wrist, blowing off his hand. But the bullet, hitting bone, was slightly deflected and instead of taking him square in the chest plowed a furrow through the flesh of his side. The impact knocked him into the front of the saloon and then to the porch floor. He lay there, his stump right in front of his eyes pumping out blood. "My god," he said in shock and horror. He could feel his strength going, feel a blackness behind his eyes. He knew he must get a tourniquet on his arm before he bled to death. With his other hand he tried weakly to wrap the surrender handkerchief around his arm just at the elbow.

They continued firing steadily at Saulter, but it was futile. He was well hidden down below his horse's body. He could hear the shells plunking into the carcass. He looked over at Letty. He was reloaded and ready. She had worked herself deeper into the snow. "Listen! When I fire you break back for the house. It's only about ten yards. And you get in there and stay there!"

She nodded.

He aimed in a pause in the firing, and put a bullet through what remained of the sash. As he fired Letty jumped up and ran. McGraw looked up just in time to see her disappear behind the house. He tried a wild shot, but it was wide. Then he dropped down as Saulter fired again.

"That bitch!" he swore. "Oh, that bitch! I'll fix her if it's the last thing I do."

Then there was a lull while both parties watched to see what the other would do. Saulter could see Billy laying on the porch up against the wall. He assumed he was dead. He lay there, his rifle at the ready, looking for movement. He'd almost been suckered and he wasn't going to let that happen again.

In the saloon, Schmidt was swearing steadily. The gunman was mumbling something. McGraw turned on him harshly. "What? What are you saying?"

"I'm just counting," the man answered sullenly. "Billy makes seven. Seven he's kilt. You tell me what our chances are. I say we get out of here."

"Shut up," McGraw told him viciously. "We go when I say."

"Listen, them horses is still out back. He's afoot now. We could take them and get clean out of the country before he could even make a start after us."

"That man dies!" McGraw screamed at him.

"I'll kill him and that bitch if it's the last thing I do! And you'll help me."

The man said, "I don't know about that, Mister McGraw. This job don't look so good now. I'd say we're out of business."

"Look here," McGraw said, peering over the windowsill. He made his voice quieter. "I believe we've got him now. He is afoot. He can't move around. We'll come at him from two sides. His dead horse will only protect him from one side. We have to get him. That rifle of his is just a single shot."

"He don't shoot it like it is."

"You take a horse and circle way behind him. I'll come from this side. If we keep our range we've got to get him."

The gunman was pensive, thinking. "That might work," he said.

"It has to. You get way around behind him. I'll come out the front door and charge him from this side. I think I can make it to the corner of the women's house. At my signal you charge. When he gets on this side of his horse I'll have a clear shot at him."

"Okay," the man said, getting up. He looked at McGraw. "But you be damn sure you do your part. You leave me charging down on him and I'm done for."

"Don't worry," McGraw said. "We get this man and you can have the other boys' payday."

"Don't forget that," the man said. He scuttled quickly across the floor and out the back door.

Up on the knoll Saulter watched. Reaching in a pocket he located the stump of a cigar. He stuck it in his mouth, found a match, and lit up, all without taking his eyes off the front of the saloon. Through a wreath of blue smoke he saw the gunman riding out, circling backwards to stay out of range.

He reached up and touched his horse's mane. It had been a good horse, his buffalo horse. No sounds came, but his lips formed the word "bastards."

McGraw had gone to the open door. Through the swirling snow he hazarded quick peeks around the jamb, watching Saulter and watching the progress of the rider.

Saulter too was watching the man, his head turning on a slow swivel. When the rider was finally behind, opposite the saloon, he stopped and waved his rifle over his head. Saulter glanced quickly toward the saloon. He could just see McGraw peeking out the door.

McGraw stuck his head out, yelled, "Now!" and fired his rifle as a signal.

The rider suddenly put spurs to his mount and, whooping and yelling, started the long charge down on the hunter. Saulter glanced quickly back toward the saloon, saw that McGraw was still inside, then deliberately came to one knee. He quickly fumbled two shells out of his satchel and put them in his mouth. He understood what they were going to try and do and it could get very tight, but he didn't think McGraw was much of a shot and he knew the man on the horse was going to have to pull up and stop before he could get off very accurate fire.

He glanced back and saw McGraw edging

around the door. As he looked McGraw threw up
his rifle and fired a couple of ineffective shots. He
swiveled his head back to Jackhammer, still
charging. The gunman was firing, but the shots
were more for show than anything else. One
whined into the snow near Saulter's knee, but he
paid it no mind. He watched the man, calculating
the distance, his mind still on McGraw behind
him.

Jackhammer too was calculating the distance
and beginning to realize he was getting awfully
close with no support. He yelled, "McGraw!
McGraw!"

Almost as if it had been his cue, Saulter whirled
at the words and threw up his rifle. He caught
McGraw starting out the door. It was a snap shot,
but it chipped splinters off the doorjamb and sent
McGraw tumbling back inside. Now knowing he
had to work rapidly, Saulter broke his rifle down,
flipped out the spent hull, and rammed home a
fresh cartridge. He snapped the rifle together and
brought it to his shoulder. Jackhammer was only
fifty yards away and suddenly aware of his danger.
He sawed backwards on the reins, trying to bring
his plunging horse to a stop in the loose snow. By
the time he was able to turn the animal he was
only thirty yards away. He rode away, spurring
and quirting the floundering animal while Saulter
took a leisurely sight in the middle of his back.
The impact of the big shell at that range knocked
the man completely over his horse's head.

Saulter quickly reloaded and turned to face the
saloon. But he was too late. It was the moment
McGraw had planned for. He had never really

intended to back up Jackhammer, but to use the situation for a diversion that would allow him to break for the women's house. He knew that once he had Letty, he had Saulter. And he wanted her almost as much as he wanted the big hunter. He was in a rage as he dashed across the open space. His men were dead, his big job was blown, and his quarter of a million dollars was gone. He ran low, sprinting hard.

It took an instant for Saulter to pick up his flying figure.

Then there was only time for a quick shot. He fired, but he knew it was futile even as the stock slammed back against his shoulder. McGraw disappeared behind the angle of the building.

"Goddammit!" he said, getting to his feet. He grabbed up his satchel of shells and began running away from the women's house, quartering up on the side of the saloon.

McGraw made the porch in one jump. He didn't bother with the door knob, but instead fired two shots into the latch and then kicked it open. He stood there for half a second grinning at the women and then kicked the door to behind him. "Now," he said to Letty, "we'll see about things. Won't we, Miss Letty?" The women stood there in the half gloom of the room looking fearful. There was such rage on his face they didn't know what he might do. But he said, "All in good time."

Then moving quickly, he raced across to a side window and hammered out the glass with his rifle butt. In a look he saw that Saulter was no longer behind his horse.

"Goddammit!" he swore.

But then he turned and looked at the women and smiled. "But I've got him just the same, haven't I, Letty?" He looked at her. "He's a gentleman, isn't he, Letty? You ought to know about that. He won't desert you here with me. Because he knows what I intend to do to you. And when he comes to your rescue, then I'll have him." He raised his rifle. "You're all the bait I'll need. The rest of you ladies get on the other side of the room and stay in a group. Stay clear of Miss Letty. She's poison. She's contagious. You don't none of you want to catch what she's going to get."

Saulter came cautiously around the back of the saloon. There were no windows in the back so he had to wait until he got to the door to look inside. At the opening he listened for a moment and then took off his hat and slid an eye just past the sill. It took a moment for his vision to adjust to the darkness of the room, but he saw that the place was empty. He stepped quickly around the sill and went cautiously into the room, his rifle at the ready. Just inside he stopped. He saw William laying behind the end of the bar and the dead man in the middle of the room and the one by the wall. He took another step and heard something to his right. He whirled. It was Schmidt, rising from behind the bar, his hands over his head. "Don't shoot!" he screamed. "For god's sake, don't shoot!"

Saulter covered him with the rifle. "Get out," he said.

Schmidt looked uncomprehending. "Get out?"

"Yes, I don't want you at my back."

"But I ain't with them."

"Get out," Saulter repeated calmly. "Or I'll blow a hole in you."

Schmidt understood. He scuttled out from behind the bar and out the door. Just as he exited Saulter stopped him. "Where's that boy? That half-breed?"

Schmidt pointed out the door. "Maybe dead. That one"—he motioned toward the dead body of William—"shot him."

"All right. Get out."

Saulter went to the door and watched Schmidt trudge across the snow and disappear into the bunkhouse. Then he stepped out the door, glanced cautiously all around, and went over to the horses that were still tied at the back. With hand and eye he carefully examined each. Finally he selected one, moved it away from the others, and tied it. The snow was starting to fall again and the horses were stamping and moving around from the cold.

A horse seen to, Saulter went back in the saloon. He stopped at the bar to pick up a bottle of whiskey, pulled the cork as he walked, and then knelt down by the window. He took a long pull of the whiskey, shuddered, and then looked cautiously toward the women's house. All was quiet. He set the bottle down, shifted his rifle to a position on the window ledge, and settled down. He knew McGraw was in the women's house; knew that he, Saulter, had control of all the horses; knew McGraw was not going to start anywhere on foot. He also knew that McGraw had Letty and that there was nothing to do but wait. The next move was up to McGraw.

It was not long in coming. From behind a window at the front of the women's house, McGraw called, "Saulter! Saulter!"

Saulter raised his head cautiously, half sighting down his rifle barrel. Finally he yelled out, "Speak up! I hear you!"

"Come out with your hands up! Now!" McGraw said.

Saulter didn't bother to answer.

"You hear me?"

Still Saulter was silent.

"Listen to me, Saulter. I got your girlfriend in here. I got a gun at her head. You walk out in that road or I'll blow her pretty face off."

Saulter yelled back, "McGraw, you got one chance. Let those women alone and ride out of here. You come out now and I won't kill you."

"Saulter! I'm not kidding you. I'll kill this woman if you don't do as I say."

"You touch her and I'll kill you twenty different ways."

"Your last chance, Saulter. I'll give you one minute to think it over."

"Last time I thought something over it cost you every man you had. This time it'll be your turn."

Inside the women's house McGraw was standing with Letty at a front window. He had her by the hair, half bent over, his pistol at her head. He had kicked the glass out of the window, but there was still a curtain over it, so that Saulter couldn't see them. But if he could he wouldn't have been able to fire for fear of hitting Letty. "You want her to beg you, Saulter?" McGraw yelled. "You want to hear from her?" He prodded Letty with the gun and shook her by the hair. "Sing, my little pigeon. Beg Mister Saulter."

She gave him such a fierce struggle that he rapped her sharply on the side of the head with his pistol barrel. "Hold still, you bitch! Now tell Saulter to save your worthless neck!"

She yelled, made half breathless from the way McGraw had her doubled over, "Saulter! Kill the bastard! Kill him!" She got no further because McGraw slapped her. Saulter heard her scream. In a strong voice he called, "McGraw, I got all the horses. You can't get away unless I let you. It's coming on dark. Walk out now and I give you my word I'll let you go." He sighted down the rifle barrel, trying to get a glimpse of McGraw, but the curtain made it impossible to see into the house.

"I got all the cards, Saulter," McGraw yelled. "I swear I'll kill her!"

Saulter glanced anxiously toward the sun. Its lower rim was just touching the horizon. Dark was near, but it was long moments away.

Letty's voice suddenly broke out. "Don't do it, Saulter. He'll kill me anyway. He'll kill you and then kill me. Just kill—"

Her voice broke off in the sounds of a struggle.

"You coming, Saulter?" McGraw yelled.

Saulter glanced toward the sun again. Twilight was full upon the snow. "She doesn't mean anything to me. Kill her if you want. I'm riding out."

"You're lying."

"Watch me! I'm heading south."

"This woman will be on your head."

"Go to hell. I'm pulling out." Saulter stood up and went to the door. "And I'm taking all the horses with me. You'll freeze to death before you can get out of here, McGraw."

"You're bluffing, Saulter."

"Watch me!"

"I'll carve her up! I'll slit her belly! I'll cut her like a sow."

"Watch me," Saulter yelled again. He turned and went out the back, glancing toward the bunk-house to make sure Schmidt was not a threat. Then he went to the horse he'd selected. He stepped aboard, and rode to where the other horses were tied. Leaning out of the saddle he gathered up the reins, turned on lead and rode around the barn and south, leading the other horses. In the open, but out of rifle shot from the women's house, he paused. Holding his big rifle in one hand he fired a signal shot in the air. There was no effect from the house. After watching a moment he kicked his horse into a lope and set off south. The sun was now down and the winter darkness coming fast. In a moment he had disappeared into the gloom.

In the women's house McGraw, still holding Letty by the hair, was craning his head out the window, watching Saulter ride away. When he was out of sight he pulled back in, looked at Letty, and then flung her away. She staggered across the floor, hit a wall, and fell down. McGraw walked deliberately to a chair and sat. The other women were huddled on the couch across the room. McGraw said to one of them, "Bring me a bottle of whiskey."

The woman got up, as if hypnotized, and hurriedly fetched the bottle of whiskey and a glass. He took them, poured a drink, and downed half of it. Then he said to the woman, "Now get to that back window and watch for Saulter. Any sight or sound of him you sing out, or I'll put your eyes out." The woman hurriedly took up her post.

McGraw slowly set his glass down and looked at the other women. "The rest of you watch. I'm going to show you what happens to a whore who doesn't stick to the business she gets paid for." He reached in his pocket and came out with a knife. With a wrist snap he flipped it open. The blade was long and sharp. He looked at Letty, his eyes bright. "Now. Come here. I'm going to skin you alive."

Saulter rode perhaps a half mile. Finally he pulled up, satisfied that he couldn't be seen from the little settlement. He dismounted and, taking a rope, made a picket line by running it though the reins of all the horses. Next he took his big rifle and, holding it by the stock, drove the barrel deep into the hard-packed snow. To this he tied the picket rope, there being nothing else to tie the horses to. In his belt was a pistol he'd taken off one of the dead gunmen in the saloon. He took it out and checked the load. Satisfied, he shoved it down in his belt. Then he tugged his hat down, pulled his big coat around him as protection against the hard cold that had come with the night, and started walking back toward the little settlement. Once he looked back. The horses were huddled together, a dark, indistinct shape against the snow.

In the women's house they were as before, the women on the sofa, McGraw in the chair, and Letty huddled at the base of the wall where McGraw had flung her. It had grown dark in the room and McGraw directed one of the women to light a candle. "Just a little one," he said, "so that I'll have light enough for my work, but not enough to make us targets for Letty's Mister Saulter." He felt very secure. He had Letty and he was inside and Saulter was somewhere in the snow. And he did not believe that Saulter could slip into the house. There was just the front door and the back. And so far as he knew, the only windows on the lower story were the two at the front and the one at the side. He knew that he could stay awake all night and once morning came Saulter would have even less chance. He would have to come for Letty soon; his whole character said he would have to. And McGraw intended on hurrying him along by a simple expedient. He looked over at Letty and smiled pleasantly, like a man with a task in front of him that he particularly relished.

"Are you coming here, Letty, or will I have to come and fetch you? I want you over in this chair so that you'll be comfortable. And nearer the window so that Mister Saulter will hear you when you scream."

She stared back, hating him, but not speaking.

"Oh, yes," he said, as if she'd answered, "he's still out there. I have no doubt of that. His avowals of departure, leaving the damsel in distress, were piteously weak. You see, I understand Mister Saulter and he's a fool. He'll come rushing blindly in through that door when you begin to scream. Make no mistake of that. He's out there and he'll come."

She lay there against the wall, watching McGraw, but frantically thinking of how she could get her hands on some weapon.

"Of course," he went on, "you think you won't scream. You think you'll be proof against such weakness. My dear madame"—he smiled broadly—"I assure you that you will scream. And loud. And you'll beg. No matter how strongly you believe now that you will not, you'll find that it will rise from your throat involuntarily. Now, are you coming here or do I have to come fetch you?"

She looked at him a long second, then she said, "Go fuck yourself."

Saulter paused some thirty yards from the women's house. It was so dark that he had to move closer to make sure that Chiffo's ladder was still leaning as he'd left it. He glanced around. The saloon was dark and empty, just a dim hulk in the moonless night, but there was a faint light from the windows of the bunkhouse. Saulter assumed it was Schmidt, hiding there until it was all settled and he had his little way station back. He moved up to the ladder, tested it with a hand, and then stood a moment listening. He could hear nothing from inside through the thick log walls.

In the parlor McGraw was having a brief struggle with Letty. He'd had to go get her, taking her by the hair, and attempting to drag he across the room. But she'd fastened onto his leg and sunk her teeth into his calf so that he'd had to punch her in the head with his fists until she'd finally fallen to the floor. "Goddam bitch!" he swore, panting with the effort. He leaned down, got her under the arms, and dragged her across to the chair he'd placed in front of the opened window. She came to as he was forcing her down and began to fight. He had to hit her until she once again slumped into submission. In the pause he grabbed up some cloths, tore them into strips, and bound her arms and legs tightly to the chair. Finished, he stood up and looked down on her, breathing heavily. She had come to and she stared back at him, her nose puffed, a line of blood running down from her mouth. She spit out a little blood, trying to spit on him, but not succeeding. "You bastard," she said, "I'll kill you. Somehow."

He smiled again, now that she was immobilized, the pleasure returning to his eyes. "Well now," he said, "I doubt that you'll get the chance." He reached out a hand, took her by the collar of her bodice, and ripped it down the front, baring her breasts. "Now we'll see how much you can take. That should be interesting." He took his long knife out of his pocket, opened it again, and tested the point against the white skin of her stomach. Even with just a little pressure it drew a tiny drop of blood. Letty turned her head and looked at the women sitting on the sofa. She said, "Won't any of you help me?"

Under her gaze they, one by one, dropped their eyes.

Letty said, "He's nothing. He's a coward. Together you could handle him."

Hester said, self-righteously, "I warned you, Letty. I warned you not to bring that man in here. Now you'll just have to take what's coming to you."

Letty shook her head slowly. "You poor bitch," she said simply. She looked back at McGraw. This time he was closer and she spit in his face. "You're nothing, McGraw. No matter how bad you hurt me it won't make you any more than nothing."

He stepped back from her, her spit on his cheek. He fumbled for his handkerchief, remembered he'd given it to Billy, and then took up one of the cloths and slowly wiped his face. "I'm glad you did that," he said, "it will increase my enjoyment of what is to come."

Saulter climbed slowly and carefully, avoiding the slightest noise. When he got to the top of the ladder the loft window was, as he'd expected, closed. He took it by the bottom and tugged up gently. It refused to budge. There was just enough of an opening at the bottom for him to slip the ends of his fingers in. He pulled up again, harder this time. It was either stuck or locked. He peered in through the glass. Just inside he could see a stick someone had put at the side of the window to jam it closed. He would have to break the glass. There was no choice. He took out his gun, reversed it, and tapped the butt gently against the pane. It made an alarmingly loud noise in the quiet night. And he would have to hit harder, making more noise, for the glass to break. He drew back his pistol. There was no help for it; it would have to be done.

Letty was cursing McGraw steadily in a low monotone. He was down on his knees in front of her with the knife in her belly. He had the blade run in just a quarter of an inch under the skin. Then he'd turned it laterally, running the supple blade between the skin and the muscle wall of her stomach. It was excruciatingly painful and Letty was strained upward against her bonds, sweat bathing her face. But her voice never broke, just stayed in the murmured cursing she was giving McGraw. The cut was so delicate and sharp that the wound was bleeding very little. He turned the blade again, slipping it, inch by inch along underneath her skin. The blade was a full five inches long and most of it had disappeared into her flesh. He worked with an intense, excited smile on his face. "Scream," he urged her, "scream and it'll feel better. Call Saulter. Beg him. Scream, Letty."

But she wouldn't. Occasionally her voice broke and a quiet, agonized "Oh, my god!" was squeezed out of her. But she was cursing loud enough so that neither McGraw nor anyone in the room heard the faint tinkle of glass as Saulter broke out the pane in the loft room upstairs.

Quickly he reached through, knocked the stick out of the way, and eased the window up. Then he climbed through, having difficulty because of his large bulk and the smallness of the window. Once in the room he stood quietly for a moment and then shrugged out of his coat and threw it on the floor. With the revolver in his hand he opened the door softly and started down the stairs. He could hear a quiet murmur from the first floor, but he didn't know what it meant.

Letty had given up cursing. She sat now with her mouth clamped shut, just using all her strength to resist the pain. McGraw stopped probing with the knife and looked up at her, puzzlement in his face. "Well, little lady," he said, "it appears we're going to have to try something else. Perhaps you are more sensitive elsewhere. Though, your profession being what it is, I have my doubts. Still we'll try." He pulled the knife out of her belly. Blood came trickling behind it. Then with rough hands, he ripped her dress the rest of the way down the front.

Saulter was at the last step. The stairwell entered in the middle of the south wall of the room. Standing motionless he could see the women on the couch to his right. They were staring raptly at something in the front of the room, completely unaware of him. He craned his head out just an inch and then he could see McGraw down in front of Letty with the knife. Now that the pain had ceased temporarily she lay with her head resting back against the chair, her face chalk white, gasping for breath.

Saulter was about to step out into the room when there came a sudden pounding at the door. He moved back half a step.

At the sound McGraw jumped to his feet and flattened himself against the wall by the door. From his belt he took out a revolver, cocking it and holding it ready.

The pounding came again. "McGraw! It's me, Schmidt! Open up."

Staying against the wall, McGraw reached out with one hand and jerked the door open. He was ready to fire when Schmidt came stumbling into the room.

"He's out there!" Schmidt said. "That wildman. I think I just saw him outside!"

McGraw turned to give Letty a triumphant leer and then went to the window and peered around the edge. It was too dark to see.

At that instant Saulter stepped out of the stairwell, revolver leveled. McGraw was turned away and did not see him. But Schmidt, who was still standing in the door, did. The fat saloon keeper's eyes bulged out and grew round and his mouth fell open. Without a word he went backpedaling out the door, staring at Saulter. At the edge of the porch he tripped and fell in the snow. Then he jumped to his feet and went racing away in the darkness.

McGraw said, "What the hell?" and turned. Then he saw Saulter, saw the revolver pointed straight at his chest. He froze. Then, almost in slow motion, his nerveless fingers, one by one, released the hold he had on his own gun and it fell to the floor. "Saulter . . ." he said. "Saulter . . ." He swallowed.

Saulter just stared at him a long moment. Then he motioned toward Letty. "Cut her loose."

"Of course. Of course," McGraw said. He grabbed up the knife that he'd left on the floor and quickly cut her bonds. She slumped down in the chair, half-unconscious. "She's not hurt," McGraw said. "Not hurt at all, really. Just a little fun. You can understand I'm sure. My position . . ."

"Yes," Saulter said. He motioned with the revolver. "Go stand in that door facing me."

"Of course," McGraw said. "Whatever you say." He stepped quickly to the open doorway and turned to face Saulter. "Do you want me to put my hands up?"

"It doesn't matter," Saulter said evenly.

Then McGraw realized. "Now wait," he said. "Wait, now. God, Saulter, don't kill me. Please don't." He put out his hands, as if to ward off the forthcoming bullet.

"You should have left me alone. All of you."

"I see that now," McGraw said rapidly. "I'm sorry. Look, Saulter, I've got money. I can get you money. You'll profit from this."

Saulter fired, shooting him in the right knee. McGraw screamed and half fell. He would have gone down except he caught himself against the doorjamb. "Oh, please," he said. "Oh, please don't."

"Get up," Saulter said. "Stand on your feet."

"I can't," McGraw cried. "I can't." Instead of rising he slid slowly down the door, his wounded leg curled under him.

Saulter shot him in the thigh.

McGraw screamed in pain and covered the wound with both hands, sliding lower.

"Get up," Saulter said. He shot him in the shoulder, the force of the shell slamming McGraw back against the corner of the door.

"Get up," Saulter said again.

Slowly, agonizingly, McGraw raised himself to

a sitting position. He held his hands out in a prayerful attitude to the hunter. "Oh, please don't, Mister Saulter. Please don't shoot me anymore."

Saulter fired, shooting him in the chest. The force of the bullet knocked him over backwards and half out the door. He twitched once and then lay still. Saulter uncocked the pistol and walked over and looked down at the dead body. Then he opened the revolver magazine and levered the spent shells out. They hit McGraw on the chest and bounced onto the floor. Finally Saulter reached down with one hand, grabbed McGraw by the coat lapels, and dragged him out on the porch and threw him over the edge into the snow. He turned back into the room, shutting the door behind him. Letty was sitting up in the chair. She'd seen the last of it. She had her clothes pulled together, but the pain was still evident in her face.

Saulter stood there looking at her. Then he rammed the revolver down his belt.

"It's over," he said.

SEVEN

THE MORNING BROKE with such brilliant clearness, as if to innocently disclaim any part of the previous night's snowstorm. Saulter got up, leaving Letty still asleep, dressed quietly, and went into the living room. From somewhere in the back of the house he could smell the coffee that Juno was fixing. Before stepping outside he lit up one of his little black cigars. He felt content. Not particularly good about what had happened, but more like a man who'd successfully completed a distasteful piece of work.

He opened the door and stepped out into the brilliant sunshine. McGraw's body lay where he'd thrown it the night before, but it was not alone. Schmidt was at it, rifling the pockets. He looked up from his work, surprise and fear in his face, when he saw the hunter. Saulter paused, smoking his cigar and studying the scene. Schmidt had a sheaf of bills in one hand and McGraw's gold watch in the other. He gestured in Guilty defiance and said, "He owed me money. I just collect what is mine. That's all."

"You do that," Saulter said. He took the cigar out of his mouth. "And since it looks as if you're being paid a little extra you can just be the burial detail." He gestured with his cigar. "Get him underground. And the rest of 'em. I don't want Letty having to see nothin' like this."

Schmidt looked aghast. "How am I gonna do that? That would be a job of work for two men. And the ground is froze!"

"Just do it," Saulter said. "Stick 'em under the snow. They'll keep until spring and then it's your problem. But you get 'em out of sight. You understand me?"

Schmidt hung his head in submission and nodded. He stuffed the money and watch in his pocket and went back to his search through McGraw's clothes. Saulter descended the steps and was going to walk by when Schmidt said, "That other one is over on the porch. He's still alive."

Saulter whirled around. "What other one?"

"That friendly one that saved you. Billy."

Saulter took the cigar out of his mouth. "He's alive?"

"Layin' on the porch."

"You left him out in the weather?"

Schmidt shrugged. "I thought you'd kill him anyway."

Saulter started to turn and then looked back. "What about that boy, Chiffo?"

Schmidt gestured. "He's in the bunkhouse."

Saulter's eyes narrowed.

"He's alive. I don't hurt him," Schmidt said hastily. "He's just shot a little bit."

Saulter threw his cigar away and turned and hurried for the front of the saloon.

Billy was laying where he'd fallen. Somehow he'd hung on through the long cold night. Though actually, the cold had been as much a factor in his favor as anything since it had thickened his blood and kept him from bleeding to death. His big coat had kept him from freezing. But he was in bad shape, white faced and very weak. Saulter knelt beside him. He put his hand on Billy's brow and the cowboy's eyelids fluttered open weakly. He tried a little smile that didn't come off.

"I got to get you inside," Saulter said. "I'm going to turn you over and pick you up."

Billy's lips moved. In a weak voice he said, "Like to give you a hand, but I'm one short."

"And lucky at that," Saulter said briefly. He glanced at the stump, amazed at the neat job of amputation the shell had accomplished. It gave his stomach a turn in spite of himself. He could see that the exposed stump had frozen, which had saved Billy a lot of pain. But he knew it was just delayed, that he would get the full share. He turned the cowboy over and picked him up. He felt surprisingly light. Schmidt watched as they passed him and went up on the porch. The door, having been ruined by McGraw, stood half open and Saulter brushed through it. Billy said, as Saulter carried him into the room, "Does this mean we're married?"

Letty was up, standing in the middle of the room drinking a cup of coffee. She looked in surprise at Saulter and his bundle. "One still alive," Saulter said. "I owe him."

She nodded quickly. "We'll put him in Hester's room. That bitch is gettin' her ass out of here today." She set her coffee cup down and led the way.

There were three beds in the room, all containing sleeping women. Letty went straight to Hes-

ter, grabbed her by the hair, and jerked her off
onto the floor. Then she turned the covers back
and helped Saulter lay Billy in the bed. Saulter
took the cowboy's boots off while Letty kicked
the frightened whore out of the room.

"We got to get that stump bandaged up," Letty
said matter-of-factly. "And get it disinfected."

"I'll leave it to you," Saulter said. He looked
down at Billy. The cowboy's eyes were open
though he looked terribly weak. Billy said, "You
blame me?"

Saulter asked, "What?"

"The surrender."

The hunter shrugged. "I guess not. It didn't
work out."

"I'll get the rest of the girls up and we'll get
started on him," Letty said. Saulter followed her
out of the room. "I got to go get that Mexican boy
over from the bunkhouse. I think he's shot too.
Can you handle him?"

Letty shrugged. "Why not? I may open up a
hospital."

"I mean, how are you feeling?"

The cuts had been just under the skin as
McGraw had followed on his plan to skin her
alive. She shrugged again. "I feel okay. Little sore
in the belly, but that's all. I'll be over it in a
week."

He studied her face. "We'll talk later."

"Yes. Let's get the mess cleaned up first."

He stayed three days to help with the cleaning
up and the nursing. Then he told Letty on his last
night that he'd be leaving in the morning. She

didn't say anything then, but got up with him and fixed his coffee and breakfast. They sat at the table together when he'd finished eating, the rest of the house sleeping. He fiddled with his coffee cup, feeling the tug of her. He knew she was thinking the same thing.

He said, "I hope you understand it will be hard for me to ride away from you, Letty." In the days they'd had together he'd abandoned his usual restraint and had talked with her freely.

"Then why do it?" she asked.

He made a motion with his coffee cup and could not answer. Instead he said, "I hate to leave you with all the wounded."

"Aw, that's nothing. I think Billy's through the worst of it now and Chiffo is up and around, as good as new. If we could just get him off that bottle." She laughed. "I think he'd be willing to get shot everyday just so he could get all the whiskey he wants."

"You still taking him back to Phoenix with you?"

"Why not? A drunken half-breed Indian will be perfect to work around a high class whorehouse in the territorial capital. Besides, I think he's got Juno knocked up."

Saulter smiled slightly. Then he said, "Billy ought to be up and around in another couple of days. He's promised to see you and the girls back to Phoenix. He's a good man and he'll look after you. You can trust him."

She smiled wryly. "I'd rather trust you . . ."

He looked down and did not reply.

She put her hand on his. "Listen, Saulter—

listen, I want you to know something. I'm not
putting you on the spot or asking anything, but I
want you to know that I'd give up whoring for
you. I'd be your wife and I'd be straight as an
arrow."

He turned his face away from her; he'd hoped
she wouldn't say it.

Because she was embarrassed, her voice turned
defiant. "And don't think that ain't a hell of an
offer. I got a good life. I live like a queen in
Phoenix. Silk sheets, French perfumes, the best
wines. I ride in a carriage and men tip their hats to
me. Yes, and I don't sleep with no range cowboys,
neither. I pick my customers."

He looked at her. She had her head back, her
nostrils slightly dilated. "It's not that, Letty," he
said kindly. "You know that."

She slumped. "Yes, I guess I do. You being what
you are. Well, I just wanted you to know."

"I have to live my way. And you, or any
woman, would complicate that." He stopped and
looked at her. "But if it were to be any
woman . . ." He left it hanging there.

She went out to his horse with him. He took a
moment checking his gear, then put a foot in the
stirrup and stepped aboard. She stood by him, one
hand resting on his thigh. "I'm gonna miss you,
Saulter," she said.

"I'm gonna miss you too, Letty."

"You big sonofabitch, I mean I'm really going to
miss you. The first time I laid eyes on you,
I . . . well, not much point in talking about it.
You got any idea where you're headed?"

He shrugged. "South. I'd like to get out of the snow awhile."

"Phoenix is south," she said.

He nodded. "I know."

"We'll be there in a week or two."

"I know," he said.

"Come by. I'll buy you a drink or something."

He smiled. Then he leaned down, while she rose on tiptoes in the snow, and kissed her very gently on the lips. "So long, Letty. I'll see you again."

"Goddam you," she said. Then she smiled. "All right. Just whenever and wherever you want. Just let me know."

He turned his horse's head and kicked the animal into a lope. The horse went willingly after several days in the barn, his breath coming steamy in the cold morning. They went on across the white plain, the horse's hooves kicking up little puffs of snow as the settlement behind them dropped away.